DOCTOR WHO CLASSICS

Two timeless adventures featuring the fourth Doctor.

THE SEEDS OF DOOM

A hostile alien plant form, a Krynoid, is brought to Britain by an eccentric botanist. The Doctor (Tom Baker) must destroy the plant before it annihilates the human race.

First broadcast on BBC Television: 31 January –
6 March 1976
Director: Douglas Camfield
Producer: Philip Hinchcliffe

THE DEADLY ASSASSIN

In a vision the Doctor (Tom Baker) sees the assassination of the President of the Council of Time on Gallifrey. He travels there to prevent the killing, only to be accused of the murder himself!

First broadcast on BBC Television: 30 October –
20 November 1976
Director: David Maloney
Producer: Philip Hinchcliffe

DOCTOR WHO CLASSICS

The Seeds of Doom

The Deadly Assassin

Based on the BBC television serials by Robert Banks Stewart
and Robert Holmes by arrangement with BBC Books, a
division of BBC Enterprises Ltd

Philip Hinchcliffe

Terrance Dicks

A STAR BOOK
published by
the Paperback Division of
W.H. ALLEN & Co. Plc

A Star Book
Published in 1989
by the Paperback Division of
W.H. Allen & Co. Plc
Sekforde House, 175/9 St John Street
London EC1V 4LL

This dual edition published 1989

Printed in Great Britain

ISBN 0 352 32416 3

Contents

I

Mystery under the Ice

Everywhere, as far as the eye could see, was a gleaming expanse of white. Moberly adjusted his goggles to counteract the glare and brushed the tiny icicles from his beard. The temperature was dropping fast, and judging from the cloud formation above the distant hills, a blizzard was brewing. Two years in the Antarctic had taught him to pay attention to such signs. He pulled his parka tightly round his face and called to another muffled figure crouched in a deep trench near by.

'Come on, Charles! The weather's turning. We've got enough samples for testing.' The other man seemed not to hear him. He was hacking furiously at something in the trench with his ice pick. Moberly dropped down beside him.

'Look,' said his companion. He pointed at a dark gourd-like object, about the size of a pineapple, embedded in the icy wall.

'What is it?' asked Moberly, his eyes widening in amazement.

'Dunno. But it's not ice,' said the man named Charles, and he carefully prised the object free. 'Bit of a mystery, eh?'

Moberly nodded. 'Let's get it back to camp and take

a proper look.' He took the strange object from Charles and climbed out of the trench. It felt curiously heavy considering its size. He placed it on the sledge and teamed up the dogs for the trek back to camp. Charles joined him a moment later and the two men set off across the icy waste, the dogs barking excitedly. A sudden squall of snow blew across the sledge as it gathered speed and the wind began to howl in the distance. Moberly shivered. Without knowing why he felt uneasy, as if the approaching blizzard carried with it a sense of impending doom.

The bright yellow huts which formed Antarctica Camp Three sat huddled in the snow at the foot of a low ridge of mountains. The huts were linked by corrugated steel tunnels which gleamed like new whenever the sun shone. Now, however, the air was dark with snow as the blizzard swept down from the mountains. Moberly and his companion, Charles Winlett, had been lucky to reach camp in time.

Inside the huts the contrast was astonishing. The specially insulated walls and ceiling kept the atmosphere at an even temperature and the overall impression was one of warmth and light. In the Laboratory, John Stevenson, the expedition's chief botanist, was carefully freeing hardened ice from the outer surface of the pod-like object. He was a pleasant, chubby man of about forty-five, with a gingery moustache and thinning hair. In his white Lab coat he had the air of a kindly dentist as he probed the pod with a metal spatula.

He stopped and turned as Winlett and Moberly entered. They had removed their outer furs and were now dressed in jeans and sweaters. Derek Moberly was a large man with a big bushy beard and a serious expression. He was a zoologist and the most recent arrival on the polar expedition, which had been in the field now for three years. Charles Winlett, a geologist, was smaller and neater with a trim beard and pale blue eyes which twinkled with good humour. Both men were in their early thirties.

Moberly crossed to the pod. 'Animal, vegetable or mineral, John?' he asked.

'Vegetable,' replied Stevenson without hesitation. 'The cutaneous creasing is unmistakable. When it's properly thawed I can confirm it with a cytology test.' He gave the pod another poke with his spatula. The ice was already melting in places to reveal a hard green casing. Stevenson stared at it, puzzled. 'How deep in the permafrost was it?' he asked.

'I'd guess about the ninth layer,' replied Winlett, 'which means it's been there at least twenty thousand years.'

There was a moment's silence as the significance of this remark sank in. All three men were experts in their field but none of them had come up against anything like this before. The pod sat still and silent, glowing strangely in the rays of the ultra-violet lamp being used to thaw it out.

'Well it looks tropical to me, like a gourd,' ventured Moberly.

'Rubbish, Derek,' said Winlett. 'If it's the late Pleistocene period it can't be tropical. It's a few million years since this part of the Antarctica was rainforest.'

'That's the accepted theory,' said Moberly. 'Discoveries like this have destroyed accepted theories before, isn't that right, John?'

Stevenson did not reply. He was staring fixedly at the pod as if in a trance. 'Something wrong?' asked Moberly, and he suddenly remembered the feeling of unease that came over him when he first handled the pod himself. Stevenson rubbed his head.

'Don't you feel it?' he said slowly. There was a hint of fear in his voice.

'Feel what?' said Winlett.

'Something odd ... strange ... as if ...' Stevenson struggled for the words, 'as if there's some kind of other presence in the room.'

Winlett laughed. 'You're imagining things, John. Must be that rice pudding you had for lunch.'

Stevenson did not smile. 'I'm not joking.' He crouched over the pod as if mesmerised by it. Winlett and Moberly exchanged glances. They had never seen Stevenson like this before. He was usually cool and level-headed, not given to wild imaginings. What had got into him? Suddenly Stevenson gave a cry and backed away from the pod. 'I know what's wrong.' His voice dropped to a whisper. 'It's alive! That thing is still alive!' He began pushing the others towards the door.

'Wait a minute,' said Winlett. 'How can you tell?'

'I don't know how, but I'm certain it's a living organism.' Stevenson spoke with total conviction. 'I'm going to transmit pictures to London. Come on.' He strode out of the room. Winlett shrugged his shoulders and followed.

Moberly remained at the door a moment, an anxious look on his face. Although he didn't like to admit it, he too found the pod worrying and somehow frightening. He glanced across at it. It lay there on the bench, silent and sinister, an unwelcome guest from the Earth's deep and hidden past.

By two o'clock that same day pictures of the pod, received direct by satellite from Antarctica, had succeeded in mystifying every botanical expert in England. Sir Colin Thackeray, Head of the World Ecology Bureau, was beginning to think he was the victim of some gigantic hoax. In desperation he had finally told his Deputy, Dunbar, to get on to a chap called the 'Doctor' who worked for UNIT (United Nations Intelligence Task Force). 'Bit of a long shot,' Sir Colin had said, but worth a try in the circumstances.'

'It was understandable why Dunbar adopted a sceptical, even sarcastic attitude to the peculiar personage who invaded his office later that afternoon.

Wearing a long red velvet coat, a broad-brimmed

11

hat, and a large multi-coloured scarf trailed over his shoulder, the Doctor hardly looked the picture of scientific eminence. Dunbar wondered if in fact this was the man Sir Colin had meant, or whether there had been some mistake. He took the photographs of the pod from the filing cabinet. 'I doubt very much if you can help us—er—"Doctor",' he began frostily. 'These pictures have baffled all the experts. The only reasonable explanation seems to be that the pod comes from some extinct species of plant.'

The Doctor sprawled into a chair, dumped his feet on Dunbar's desk and beamed a large, friendly smile. 'It is the sign of a tiny mind to look for reasonable explanations, Mr Dunbar. The Universe is full of *un*-reasonable things, only capable of being explained *un*-reasonably.' Dunbar looked uncomfortable at this challenge to the normal processes of thought. 'Consider for a moment,' continued the Doctor, 'the alternative hypothesis.' He waved his arm airily.

'Such as,' snapped Dunbar, beginning to feel irritated.

'That the pod may have originated in outer space?' The Doctor smiled sweetly as if no one but a fool could possibly think otherwise.

Dunbar angrily thrust the photographs at the Doctor. 'If you have ever seen anything like this, you must have a very powerful telescope,' he said tartly. The Doctor pushed back the brim of his hat and studied the photographs. For the first time Dunbar noticed how blue and penetrating were the Doctor's eyes, and he could not help feeling he was in the presence of a very strange and powerful person, so strange he seemed not quite human.

The Doctor tossed the photos back on the desk. 'Mr Dunbar, how long is it since there was vegetation in Antarctica?'

Dunbar explained this was something the World Ecology expedition was trying to establish. The pod had been found deep in the permafrost, twenty or thirty thousand years under the ice.

'Yes, and it's probably still ticking,' interrupted the Doctor. He leapt out of his chair and headed for the door.

'What? I don't understand . . .'

The Doctor stabbed the air with his forefinger. 'A time bomb, Mr Dunbar, a time bomb! Are you in touch with the expedition?'

Dunbar nodded. 'A daily video link.'

'Good. Tell them to keep a constant guard on this pod but not to touch it under any circumstances until I arrive.'

'You're going out there?' said Dunbar, overcome by the sudden turn of events.

The Doctor bobbed his head back in. 'Just as soon as I've picked up my assistant and a toothbrush. And remember—no one must touch that pod!' Before Dunbar could reply again the Doctor had disappeared, like a vanishing rabbit in a conjuring trick.

Dunbar shook his head in disbelief. The last few

minutes had been so unlike the ordered calm which usually prevailed in his office, that he was half inclined to doubt whether the preceeding interview had really taken place at all. Finally he crossed to his desk and dialled a number on the intercom. 'Sir Colin? ... Dunbar here,' he said. 'That chap you called in from UNIT ... is he quite sane?'

It was the middle of the night at Antarctica Camp Three. The blizzard had begun to subside but the wind still whined around the huts. Winlett was sitting in the Laboratory near the pod, dozing. The room was in darkness, save for the eerie glow of the ultra-violet lamp. A half empty mug of cocoa stood on the bench where Winlett had left it before falling asleep. Now he was slumped awkwardly in his chair a few feet away. Earlier that day Stevenson had measured the pod and found to everyone's amazement that it had grown five centimetres in circumference. He had immediately ordered a round-the-clock vigil to monitor its progress. Winlett knew that such growth defied all normal biological laws. The pod had no root system to feed with and no nitrogen intake. It was odd, and disturbing. He had wondered whether Stevenson was right to continue the ultra-violet radiation in view of the warning from London, but Stevenson had brushed these fears aside.

A distant door banged shut with the wind and Winlett stirred. Still half-asleep, he shifted his position in the chair, bringing an arm to rest on the bench not far from the pod. Then he dozed off again.

Suddenly, with no sound whatsoever, the pod began to vibrate and tiny cracks appeared in the outer casing. It was opening! Winlett remained asleep and unaware.

From the top of the pod emerged a green tendril, like the shoot of some exotic plant. It reared several feet in the air then slowly turned its head, like a deadly snake seeking its victim. Seconds later it sensed the presence of another living creature in the room. Gradually, the tendril crept towards Winlett. Then, in one quick motion, it engulfed his arm. Winlett jerked awake with a cry of pain. In blind panic he reeled across the room clutching his arm. The tendril had detached itself from the pod and was clinging to him.

'John! Derek!' he shouted desperately, but a strange, cold sensation was already rushing through his body. He felt weak, his knees crumpled, and a terrible darkness descended in his brain.

2

Death Stalks the Camp

After his interview with the Doctor, Dunbar did not go straight home. Instead, he drove thirty miles out of London, taking particular care he was not followed, to pay a visit on someone very special.

'Mr Richard Dunbar, sir, of the World Ecology Bureau.' The butler threw open a pair of metal studded doors and Dunbar entered the room.

'Room' was hardly the word to describe the place he now found himself in. Dunbar literally gasped with shock at the sight. For all around him, on each side, were nothing but plants—plants of every description; creepers, suckers, lichen, fungi, giant rubber plants, monstrous cacti, rare tropical blossoms, trailing vines, bamboo—the room was a living jungle, a Sargasso Sea of waving green. Dunbar guessed it must be at least fifty yards long, although the farthest walls were invisible. High above, he could just make out a vaulted ceiling through the thick foliage.

A raised iron walkway ran down the centre of the room and at the far end a man was spraying an exotic-looking flower with loving care. He was dressed immaculately in a dark Savile Row suit, and his hands were covered by elegant black leather gloves.

The man turned as the butler made his announcement and glided down the catwalk towards Dunbar. He stopped and stared, without speaking. His eyes were extraordinarily large, like those of a predatory cat.

'Mr Chase?' said Dunbar. 'Mr Harrison Chase?'

The man nodded. There was something menacing about him. Lean and panther-like, he had the unmistakable stamp of power. A man not to be trifled with. A man who would stop at nothing to get his own way.

He spoke. 'And what is your Bureau doing about bonsai?'

'Bonsai?'

'Mutilation and torture, Mr Dunbar. The hideous Japanese practice of miniaturising shrubs and trees.'

'We try to conserve all animal and plant life,' replied Dunbar hurriedly.

'I'm glad to hear it.' The cat's eyes flashed dangerously. 'I consider it my mission in life to protect the plant life of Mother Earth. And she needs a protector, does she not?'

Dunbar agreed. He knew of this man's obsession with plants, knew too that he was a millionaire many times over, with a considerable private army in his employ. It was wiser to agree than disagree with such a man. He fumbled with his briefcase and took out a large buff envelope.

'I have come to show you something, Mr Chase, something discovered by one of our expeditions.' He undid the envelope and handed over the photographs. 'A mysterious, unidentified pod.'

Chase examined the photographs. 'Very interesting. Where was it found?'

Dunbar hesitated. This was the moment he had been waiting for, the moment he would gamble not only his career but, if the rumours about Chase were true, perhaps even his life.

'In the Antarctic, under our control,' he replied finally. 'But of course, in our violent and uncertain world, Mr Chase, anything can happen ...' he paused. 'Such a valuable specimen could easily disappear ... for a price.' He looked hesitantly into the dark, feline eyes.

'I want the precise location.'

Dunbar reached into his case again. 'A map and all the information you require.'

Chase smiled. 'Such forethought, Mr Dunbar. An excellent attribute, and one for which you will be well rewarded.' He clapped his hands. 'Hargreaves, call Scorby in here, and show Mr Dunbar out.'

The butler bowed wordlessly and ushered Dunbar into the corridor. The audience was over.

Alone, Chase stared hungrily at the photographs once more. 'Unique! The only plant of its kind in the world,' he whispered. 'Compositae Harrison Chase! Yes, I must have it. I must!' The cat-like eyes gleamed bright and manic.

A noise at the door broke the spell.

'You wanted me, Mr Chase?' The speaker was a tall, swarthy man with a pointed black beard.

'Yes, Scorby. I'm sending you on a little errand.

You'd better take Keeler with you. Oh, and wrap up well. It could be snowing.'

Sarah Jane Smith had never felt so cold in her life. She was already regretting this mad trip to Antarctica. After two years as the Doctor's special assistant she should have known better, she told herself.

She drew the hood of her parka tight and glanced across at the Doctor. He remained impassive, staring out of the helicopter window. He was being unusually secretive about their mission. A sure sign he was worried, decided Sarah.

Suddenly the pilot yelled above the engine noise. 'There she is!'

The helicopter began to turn and drop. Beneath them Sarah could just make out a huddle of bright yellow huts. So this was Antarctica Camp Three. Not exactly the centre of civilisation.

They landed and Sarah leapt out after the Doctor. The big blades swirled dangerously overhead, creating a miniature snowstorm. A figure ran out from one of the huts to greet them.

'Welcome to the loneliest spot on Earth. You must be the Doctor. We were expecting someone a lot older.'

The Doctor smiled. 'I'm only seven hundred and forty-nine. I used to be even younger.'

The man grinned, not knowing how to take this remark. He turned to Sarah and extended a hand. 'Derek Moberly, how do you do?'

'Sarah Jane Smith, the *young* Doctor's assistant,' she laughed. 'Tell me, is the weather always like this? I feel I've got frostbite already.'

Moberly chuckled. 'No, sometimes it gets quite warm. Ten degrees below freezing.' He eyed the Doctor's red velvet frock-coat. 'Are you all right dressed like that?'

'I haven't travelled ten thousand miles to discuss the weather,' snapped the Doctor. 'Shall we get started?'

A few minutes later he stood next to Stevenson in the Sick Bay, gazing down at the motionless form of Winlett.

'He hasn't spoken a word since last night,' explained Stevenson anxiously. 'We heard a cry, came in and found him on the Laboratory floor. The pod was open.'

The Doctor glanced at the progress chart and raised an eyebrow in surprise. 'According to these figures he should be dead.' He pulled back the bedclothes.

Stevenson gasped in horror. 'Good grief! What is it?'

Winlett's right hand had completely vanished and in its place was a green, vegetable-like growth.

'Whatever came out of that pod has obviously infected him,' replied the Doctor grimly. 'How soon can you get a proper medical team here?'

Stevenson tugged at his moustache. 'We've been on to them, but conditions are bad. Maybe tomorrow.'

The Doctor straightened the bedclothes and stepped back. 'I doubt if tomorrow is going to be soon enough. Show me the pod.'

20

Stevenson led him out of the Sick Bay and down a narrow, corrugated steel tunnel to a door marked 'Laboratory'. Inside, Sarah and Moberly were huddled over a crackling radio set.

'What is it?' asked Stevenson.

'Bad news,' said Moberly gravely. 'The medical team has turned back. One of their Snocats fell into a crevasse.'

Stevenson began to panic. 'What are we going to do? Winlett's dying.'

'No he's not,' said the Doctor. 'He's changing form, which could be worse. We need a blood test. Fast.'

'I'm a zoologist. I can prepare a specimen slide,' offered Moberly.

The Doctor nodded. 'Right.' Moberly hurried out and the Doctor turned to Stevenson. 'The pod?'

Stevenson led him to the bench where the pod had lain open and untouched since the attack on Winlett. The Doctor stooped to examine it. 'Why did it open, I wonder?' he muttered to himself.

Stevenson shifted uneasily. 'That could be my fault. I used the ultra-violet lamp to thaw it out. I felt certain there was life there, you see.'

The Doctor rose and gave him a stony stare. 'Mr Stevenson,' he said slowly and deliberately, 'what you have done could result in the total destruction of life on this planet.'

In the Sick Bay Winlett was growing worse by the

minute, as the green infection crept relentlessly up his arm.

Meanwhile, the Doctor had asked to see the trench where the pod had been found. For over an hour, he, Stevenson and Sarah had battled through a howling gale to reach the spot. Now he was digging furiously in the icy wall with a small pick, oblivious to the biting wind and thick snow which almost blotted the other two from view.

Suddenly he stopped. 'Yes, I thought so. Here we are.' He threw the pick aside and, scrabbling with his bare hands, lifted out of the ice a second pod, an exact replica of the first.

'Another pod!' gasped Sarah.

'How did you know . . .' began Stevenson. 'Will there be any more?'

'No. They always travel in pairs. Like policemen.' The Doctor stood up, clearly very pleased with himself.

'What are we going to do with it?' asked Sarah, puzzled.

'Put it in the fridge. Come on.' The Doctor scrambled out of the trench. The other two followed, none the wiser.

It was almost nightfall by the time they regained Camp. The Doctor immediately placed the pod in a special freeze box in the Lab, used for keeping ice samples. There was no further news of the medical team but Moberly had taken the blood test. One look confirmed the Doctor's suspicions. The platelets of

Winlett's blood—magnified a thousandfold—revealed the presence of plant bacteria.

'As I thought,' said the Doctor, removing his eye from the microscope, 'a human being whose blood is turning into vegetable soup!'

At that moment the roar of an aircraft engine shook the walls of the Crew Quarters where they were standing.

'The medical team!' cried Sarah jubilantly.

'Quick, Derek, the landing lights!' yelled Stevenson, and the two of them grabbed their snowsuits and dashed outside.

Sarah turned to the Doctor. 'Will they be able to do anything for that man?'

'I don't know, Sarah. He's half way towards becoming a Krynoid.'

'Krynoid?'

The Doctor nodded.

'You mean you recognised the pod?'

'Oh yes,' said the Doctor. 'I was fairly certain when I saw the photographs in London. But now I'm sure.'

'Well, what is a Krynoid?' demanded Sarah, peeved he had not told her of his suspicions. 'What does it do?'

'You could describe it as a galactic weed,' explained the Doctor. 'The pod we found is just one of a thousand seeds dispersed by the mother plant. Given the right conditions, each pod releases a parasitic shoot which attaches itself to the nearest animal life-form—in this instance it happened to be human. The infected

23

victim changes rapidly and ultimately develops into a fully grown Krynoid, thus completing the cycle.'

Sarah gasped. 'But that's terrifying! How did these pods manage to land here on Earth?'

'Good question,' said the Doctor, tapping the side of his nose. 'I wish I knew the answer. Possibly their planet of origin is very turbulent. Every so often there could be internal explosions which send surface matter shooting off into space.' He paused, as if weighing up the pros and cons of the theory in his mind.

The door burst open at this point and Moberly and Stevenson struggled in, supporting two frozen, semi-collapsed figures.

'Is this the medical team?' asked the Doctor.

'Afraid not,' gasped Stevenson as he helped ease the two strangers gently into a couple of chairs. 'Just got themselves lost.'

Moberly administered some piping hot coffee from a flask, which the two men gratefully gulped down.

'Sorry to be such a nuisance,' said one of them finally. 'We were running low on fuel when we saw your lights.' He was tall and swarthy, with a black pointed beard.

'That was lucky,' said Sarah. 'Lights are few and far between in Antarctica.'

The Doctor's voice, urgent and decisive, cut through these explanations. 'The medical team was our last chance. Now we must act for ourselves. And quickly.' He shot out of the room.

'Where's he going now?' asked Stevenson.

'Where do you think?' replied Sarah. 'Come on.' She hurried out, Stevenson and Moberly close behind her.

Left alone, the two strangers exchanged wary glances.

'Do you think they swallowed it?' said the second man. He was small and ferrety.

'Don't worry, Keeler,' said the dark one. 'What can they do?' He tapped his left breast and grinned. The bulge of an automatic pistol could just be seen beneath his nylon snowsuit.

The Doctor was already in the Sick Bay when Sarah and the others rushed in. They were totally unprepared for the sight which hit them. Winlett lay on the bed, deathly pale, his breath rasping and distorted. The plant-like infection now covered his entire right side.

Stevenson fought for words. 'It's ... it's as if he's turning into some kind of monster!'

'That's exactly what is happening,' said the Doctor gravely.

'Can't we do anything to help?'

'Yes, but it's drastic,' warned the Doctor. 'We can amputate the arm. It's his only chance.'

'But none of us are surgeons,' protested Moberly. 'It could be fatal.'

'It's a risk we have to take,' snapped the Doctor. 'Come on!' He led the way out.

The door shut on the motionless form in the bed.

For a few seconds everything remained still as the footsteps receded up the corridor. Then, slowly, the figure of Winlett sat up, his head swivelled trance-like towards the door, and the glazed lifeless eyes stared murderously out of their sockets.

In the Lab the Doctor was issuing orders. 'Sarah, we'll need hot water and towels! Stevenson, get more lights. Moberly, you have some medical training. You can perform the actual surgery.'

Moberly nodded and started to gather equipment and instruments on to a tray. The Doctor glanced at the clock above the door. Every second was vital. Not only Winlett's life was at stake. Once the Krynoid organism was allowed to take root in one person, it was merely a matter of time before the whole of humanity fell prey to the lethal weed.

Moberly finished his preparations and made for the door. 'I'll take these to the Sick Bay and start setting up.'

'Good man,' said the Doctor.

Sarah glanced anxiously in his direction. 'Do you think there's a chance?'

'There's always a chance,' said the Doctor quietly, but Sarah could tell he was worried.

Moberly walked carefully down the tunnel. The Doctor was right, they would need more lights. He hoped Stevenson could fix the transformer or some-thing. He turned the corner near the Sick Bay. That was odd! The door was open. He crept forward the last few paces and peered in. The bed was empty.

'Charles?' There was no reply. 'Charles, where are you?'

Moberly stepped into the room and put down the tray. As he did so something strange and cold, like a piece of wet seaweed, touched the back of his neck. He spun round. A hideous, semi-human shape lunged at his throat and started to throttle him. Gasping, Moberly sank to his knees. The pressure increased. He couldn't breathe! The room began to spin, everything was going blurred, he could not escape from the suffocating grip! Then, nothing but blackness, rushing and overwhelming ...

Moberly fell to the floor, dead. The dark, monstrous shape rose from his body, glided like a phantom down the murky passage and slipped into the howling, stormy night outside.

3

Hunt in the Snow

Carrying an armful of towels and fresh linen, Sarah made her way towards the Sick Bay. As she drew near she suddenly felt a cold draught around her feet. Someone must have left an outside door open. She turned the corner and froze with horror. There, slumped in the shadows, lay the body of Moberly. One glance was enough to tell her the worst. She spun round. The door at the far end of the passage was banging on its hinges in the wind and snow had started to drift in. She shut the door and hurried back to the Lab.

'Moberly's dead.' Sarah stood framed in the doorway, white as a ghost.

'What?' cried Stevenson.

The Doctor threw aside the tray of bottles he was preparing and darted out. In two seconds he was by the body. There was a faint green mark under the chin. 'I found an outside door open,' said Sarah. 'Something must have come in.'

'No, Sarah,' said the Doctor chillingly. ' Something went out.'

He entered the Sick Bay. The bed lay empty and all around were clear signs that a struggle had taken place.

Stevenson shook his head. 'You don't mean Charles ...'

'... left after killing Moberly,' finished the Doctor. 'Only he is no longer Charles. He is an alien.'

'An alien? I can't believe it,' cried Stevenson in anguish.

'I told you he was changing form. Already his mind has been taken over. Eventually his entire body will alter.'

'Into a Krynoid?' said Sarah.

The Doctor nodded and turned to Stevenson. 'Winlett as you knew him is already dead. For the sake of the rest of humanity we must destroy what he has become.' He spoke gently but with finality.

Stevenson lowered his eyes, believing but not wanting to accept this terrible truth.

In the Crew Quarters the stranger with a beard was methodically searching the room. He found a rifle under one of the bunks and began to dismantle it.

'What are you doing, Scorby?' His companion spoke nervously.

'I don't like guns ... in the wrong hands.' Scorby tampered with the firing pin for a few minutes and, satisfied the mechanism was sabotaged, replaced the rifle carefully under the bunk.

'I wish you'd stop acting like some cheap gangster. We've only come here to confirm the pod is something unusual.'

Scorby grinned. 'You don't think we're going to fly back empty-handed, do you, Keeler?'

The small man looked genuinely surprised. 'It's the first you've mentioned ... what are you planning?'

Scorby gave a nasty leer. 'Tomorrow we dig a nice big hole in the snow—big enough for, say, five bodies. Then we fill the hole, take the pod and go home ... No witnesses, nothing. Just another lost expedition.'

Keeler recoiled in disgust. 'You're mad! I won't do that!'

'You'll do exactly as you're told,' Scorby tapped his pistol threateningly, 'or else ... I'll just make that hole a little bigger.'

Keeler backed away and nearly collided with the Doctor as he came hurtling in, followed by Sarah and Stevenson.

'Come on! We don't have much time,' the Doctor sounded impatient. Sarah and Stevenson hurriedly donned their snowsuits.

'What's the trouble?' asked Scorby, quickly regaining his composure.

'We're going out.'

'In this weather?'

'Yes, in this weather,' snapped the Doctor.

Stevenson crossed to his bunk and took out the rifle. 'Ready!'

The Doctor eyed the weapon. 'I hope that's the answer,' he said quietly, and led the way out.

Keeler turned anxiously on Scorby as the door slammed. 'What the devil's going on?'

'I don't know. They're not going to build a snow-

man, that's for sure.' He stepped over to the door.
'Come on. Now's our chance.'

'What do you mean?'

'To find the pod.' He opened the door gently and,
checking the corridor was clear, beckoned Keeler to
follow.

Outside, it was very dark and a heavy snow was falling.
Sarah noticed that although they had only travelled
a few hundred yards the lights of the camp behind
them were no longer visible. She shivered. The cold
was already unbearable and constant flurries of snow
prevented her from seeing more than a few feet ahead.
She stumbled on behind the Doctor. He seemed oblivious to the conditions, pausing only once in a while
to secure his hat. All the time he was scanning the
endless expanse of snow.

'No sign of any tracks,' yelled Sarah.

Stevenson shook his head. 'The wind covers everything in a matter of minutes.'

Suddenly the Doctor pointed. 'What's that over
there?' They had reached a high ridge and he was
gazing at something below.

Stevenson peered into the gloom. 'That's our Power
Unit.' A small metal building lay half-buried in the
snow, several hundred yards distant. Only the Doctor's
superhuman eyesight could have picked it out from
such a range.

'Why is it so far from the camp?' he shouted.

'Safety measure. It's a new Fuel-Cell system. Being tested out here for the first time.'

'Let's take a look!'

They scrambled down the ice-covered slope and approached the Power Unit. The snow seemed undisturbed.

'This door can't have been opened for weeks,' remarked Sarah. 'It's iced solid.'

'It's as well to be sure,' said the Doctor and he started to yank it open. 'He'd try to find shelter in this weather.' Stevenson slipped the safety catch on his rifle. After a couple of hefty pulls from the Doctor the ice cracked away and the three of them stepped inside.

The walls and floor of the Power Unit were bare, but in the centre stood a large complicated structure, about ten feet across, giving out a soft glow of heat. This was the experimental Fuel Cell. One or two large pipes and cables ran off to the walls and then underground to the rest of the camp, to supply the power and electricity needed. There was very little scope for concealment.

'No cactus spines or puddles of snow,' said Sarah. 'Doesn't look like he's been here.'

'Is there anywhere else he could hide?' the Doctor asked Stevenson.

'Not outside the camp itself.'

'He wouldn't last long, would he ... outside?' ventured Sarah.

'Not without special clothing,' replied Stevenson.

'No, I'm afraid Charles must have collapsed some-where.'

'You keep forgetting, Stevenson—he isn't a man any more. Not of flesh and blood.'

'Well, if he's a plant, Doctor—or a vegetable, what-ever he is—he'd have even less resistance to cold, wouldn't he?' argued Sarah.

'Perhaps. On the other hand, the Krynoid might come from a planet where this would be considered glorious summer.'

Stevenson frowned. 'You know, I still find this hard to take. You're trying to tell me these things are an alien plant species?'

'And lethal to all human and animal life.'

'But how do you know?'

'Never mind how I know, it's fact. On every planet where the Krynoid gets established all animal life is extinguished. What happened to your friend Moberly should convince you.' Sarah could see the Doctor was irritated by Stevenson. She tried to sound reassuring.

'But there's no real danger now, is there? One pod is safely in the freezer and ...' she was about to say 'Winlett' but checked herself, 'and ... the other ... is probably frozen stiff under the snow.'

The Doctor crossed to the door. 'I hope you're right, Sarah,' he said as he led them out.

The three figures emerging from the Power Unit were unaware of a hideous form crouched behind a snowbank, less than twenty feet away. Its cold, inhuman eyes followed the Doctor's movements as he bolted the door from the outside. Then, as the trio climbed back up the ridge and out of sight, the creature—half man, half plant—crept from hiding and crawled across the snow towards the building. With one swift movement it prised open the door and entered. Inside, it let out a low rattling noise and settled beside the fuel cell, sucking in the warmth.

In the Laboratory, Scorby and Keeler were conducting a methodical search.

'You're supposed to be the botanist, Keeler. Where would you keep this pod?'

'It must be here somewhere.' Keeler looked round in desperation. Scorby picked up an intricate piece of measuring equipment and held it aloft. 'Careful!' warned his companion, 'that's valuable.'

Scorby grinned, then smashed it violently on to the floor. 'So what?' he sneered, 'there'll be nobody here to use it after we leave.'

Suddenly the radio sprang to life. 'HELLO ... HELLO ... THIS IS SOUTH BEND CALLING CAMP THREE ... COME IN CAMP THREE ... OVER ...'

Scorby darted a look at Keeler then crossed to the radio. He pressed a switch. 'Camp Three receiving you ... over.'

'IS THAT YOU DEREK?' said the voice, distorted by static.

Scorby hesitated. 'Er ... yes ... go ahead, South Bend.'

The voice continued. 'THE WEATHER'S CLEARING THIS END. THE MEDICAL TEAM WILL BE WITH YOU AS SOON AS POSSIBLE.'

'Have they left yet?' asked Scorby, concealing his alarm.

'THEY'RE LEAVING RIGHT NOW.'

'Cancel them!' ordered Scorby. 'We don't need help. Everything's under control.'

There was silence for a moment, then the voice spoke again, this time inquisitive and suspicious. 'HELLO? ... IS THAT YOU DEREK?'

Smiling, Scorby clicked off the radio and began smashing the circuits with the butt of his gun. Keeler looked up in alarm.

'What are you doing?'

'Fixing it,' grinned Scorby. 'Didn't anyone ever tell you, silence is golden?'

'But ...'

'Shut up, Keeler, and find that pod!' The small man winced as his partner savagely dismembered the radio equipment.

A few moments later, however, Keeler let out an excited yell as he removed a tray from under the bench. On it lay the two empty halves of the first pod.

Look! It's the pod in Dunbar's photograph.' He fitted the two halves together.

'Some idiot's cut it open,' hissed Scorby.

Keeler shook his head. 'No. It wasn't cut. It must have germinated.'

'What's that?'

'The pod has opened as part of its natural cycle to release a shoot or something.'

Scorby digested this unexpected piece of information. 'But it's the actual *plant* that Harrison Chase wants, right?'

'Right.'

'Then what have they done with it, Keeler?' He paced the room nervously. 'We've got to find it or Chase'll skin us alive!'

'If you hadn't smashed the radio perhaps we could have asked South Bend.'

Scorby gave Keeler a scornful look. 'Are you trying to be funny? The discovery of this pod has been kept secret. Only the top brass of the Ecology Bureau know about it.'

'And Harrison Chase,' corrected Keeler.

'That bloke on the radio said medical aid was coming. Medical aid for who? There must be someone here who's ill.' A malevolent smile settled on his dark features. 'And he'll tell us where this thing is, I promise you.'

Gun in hand, Scorby led the way out of the Lab and down the passage. It ran to an intersection.

'Which way?' whispered Keeler.

Scorby paused then headed to his left. On the floor at the far end of the tunnel was a towel dropped earlier by Sarah in her haste. The two men turned the corner.

Opposite was a door marked 'Sick Bay'. Scorby smiled and pushed open the door. His expression immediately turned to shock as he caught sight of a body on the bed, hurriedly draped in a sheet.

'Is he dead?' gasped Keeler.

Scorby pulled back the sheet. 'Stiff as a board.'

'Look! What's that?' Keeler's finger pointed to the green mark on Moberly's throat.

'Dunno. But it's not measles.' Scorby twitched the sheet back. 'And he won't be telling us anything either.'

At that moment they both heard a noise in the corridor outside. Footsteps and voices were approaching. Scorby signalled Keeler to go behind the door and quickly positioned himself at the other side. It sounded like the Doctor and that girl. They were bound to notice the open door. Scorby's finger tightened on the trigger of his gun.

The Doctor paused outside the Sick Bay, puzzled. Something was wrong. He motioned to Sarah to keep quiet. Why was the door open? His mind raced through the events of the last few hours like a computer. The two strangers! Of course! Their landing here was too much of a coincidence. They had come with a purpose, and that could mean only one thing!

The Doctor sprang into the room ... and Scorby's pistol dug coldly into his neck.

4

Sabotage!

'Put your hands up, Doctor!'

The Doctor obeyed.

'And you!'

Sarah was yanked into the room and forced to follow suit.

The Doctor eyed the gun. 'Have we annoyed you in some way? Food not to your liking?'

'Shut up!' commanded Scorby viciously. 'OK ... now start talking.'

'Make up your mind,' smiled the Doctor.

'I said talk.'

'Certainly. Did you know that Wolfgang Amadeus Mozart had perfect pitch?'

Sarah could see Scorby was not amused.

'What happened to him?' he hissed, jerking his head towards the bed.

'Wolfgang Amadeus?' The Doctor feigned puzzlement. 'Oh, *him*,' suddenly serious. 'He died.'

'We gathered that.'

'What did it?' asked Keeler.

The Doctor did not answer.

'It's something to do with that pod, isn't it? What's happened to the pod?'

'What pod?'

The pistol dug deeper into the Doctor's neck.

'There's already one corpse in here, Doctor. I can easily double that number.'

Sarah glanced anxiously at the Doctor out of the corner of her eye. She felt certain Scorby meant what he said.

Finally the Doctor spoke. 'There's been an accident. One of the men here has been ... infected.'

'By the pod?' exclaimed Keeler.

'He went mad,' said Sarah quietly.

'Yes,' added the Doctor, 'you could say he's not quite himself anymore.'

'Where is he now?'

'We don't know,' answered Sarah. 'Somewhere out there.'

Keeler glanced around nervously. 'You mean you have a homicidal maniac on the loose?'

'More dangerous than that, I'm afraid,' replied the Doctor. 'If he ... or rather it, is still alive, then it will be desperate to reach food and warmth. And there's only one place it can find these things.' He weighed his words carefully and looked for their effect on the two strangers.

'You mean this Camp?'

'Yes, comforting thought, isn't it?' said the Doctor airily. 'I advise you to keep all doors and windows locked. That is, if you're planning to stay.' He smiled sweetly, like a benevolent hotel proprietor.

Keeler looked anxiously at his partner. 'What are we going to do?' Sarah could see the other man was not convinced.

'I want some more answers. But not in here.' Scorby nodded towards the bed. 'He gives me the creeps. Come on, you two. *Move!*' He prodded the Doctor and Sarah out of the Sick Bay and into the corridor.

In the Power Unit the creature was growing stronger by the minute, bathed by the warm glow from the Fuel Cell. All vestige of humanity had long since disappeared and it was now a mass of tendrils and fibrous shoots, like some giant, malformed plant; but a plant that could move and crush and kill. Slowly, it began to stir. From where the green growth was thickest there came a strange, low rattling sound. Then, the whole monstrous shape started to creep towards the door.

The Doctor and Sarah were led into the Crew Quarters and bound hand and foot on the floor. So far the two men seemed to have forgotten about Stevenson, who was busy locking the doors and windows of the outer huts. The Doctor wondered how long it would be before he returned. Stevenson still had his rifle with him. If they could play for time ... He became aware of Scorby's pistol again.

'Right, Doctor, let's have the truth. Where's the plant that came out of that pod?'

'That grew in the bed that was part of the house that Jack built?'

'I am not a patient man,' threatened Scorby.

Suddenly Keeler interrupted. 'Ssshh! Hold it. Someone's coming. Must be the other guy.'

Scorby turned from the Doctor and pointed his gun at the closed door.

'Doctor? Miss Smith? Where are you?' came a voice from outside.

The door opened and Stevenson entered.

'Come and join the party.' Scorby lowered his pistol to wave the visitor in. Stevenson reacted like lightning and fired his rifle point blank at Scorby's chest. There was a harmless click.

Scorby chuckled. 'Not very friendly.' He grabbed Stevenson by the shoulders and hurled him across the room. 'Get over there!' Stevenson fell with a crunch beside the others.

'Good try,' said the Doctor.

'What's happening?'

'For some reason these two want to get their hands on the pod.' He looked meaningfully at Stevenson. 'I've told them how dangerous ...'

'The pod's still safe?' interrupted Stevenson, misunderstanding. 'They haven't taken it out?'

Scorby's ears pricked up visibly and Stevenson realised his blunder.

'Taken it out where?' Scorby turned to Keeler, a look of triumph on his face. 'Know what that means?'

Keeler grinned. 'They've got a second pod!' Stevenson shot the Doctor an anguished look.

Scorby crossed to them both. 'Where is it?'

'Don't be a bigger fool than you already are,' said the Doctor angrily. 'Don't you understand, it's dangerous!'

'Where is the pod?'

The gun pointed menacingly at them, but the Doctor and Stevenson remained mute.

'Stubborn pair, aren't they,' said Scorby, controlling his venom. 'All right ...' He put the pistol against Sarah's head. 'I mean it this time,' he whispered softly. Sarah felt her stomach turn over. She held her breath for what seemed an eternity.

The Doctor's voice broke the silence. 'It's in the freezer.'

'Thank you, Doctor.' Scorby took out a second, smaller pistol, which he handed to Keeler. 'Watch them. You,' he prodded Stevenson, 'come with me.' He bundled the unhappy scientist out of the room.

Keeler trained the gun nervously on the Doctor and Sarah. 'Don't worry,' beamed the Doctor. 'You're quite safe with us.'

Stevenson led Scorby to the Lab and produced the second pod out of the freezer.

Scorby cursed Keeler under his breath for missing it. 'Are there any more?'

'No. This is unique—priceless—as you are no doubt aware.'

'What's to stop it breaking open like the other one?'

'It's quite safe at this temperature,' replied Stevenson calmly.

'I see. Well, it's going on a little journey, so find me something to keep it cool.'

Stevenson hunted round the debris until he found a thermo-container in which he placed the pod. As they returned to the Crew Quarters, Scorby asked about their source of electrical supply. Stevenson explained curtly about the Power Unit.

When they rejoined the others, Stevenson was bound hand and foot like the Doctor and Sarah.

'You can say your goodbyes now,' sneered Scorby and pointed his gun at the helpless captives.

'You're not going to shoot us in cold blood?' murmured Sarah.

With a laugh Scorby let his arm drop. 'No. I've got a better idea.' He grabbed hold of Sarah. 'You're coming with us. Give me a hand, Keeler.' Sarah's feet were untied and she was dragged towards the door.

'How do you expect to get away from here?' yelled Stevenson. 'You said your plane was grounded.'

Scorby smiled. 'You shouldn't believe everything people tell you.' With a bang the door slammed shut.

Sarah, her hands still tied, was led to an outer door.

'Right,' ordered Scorby. 'Take us to the Power Unit.'

'I don't know where you mean,' lied Sarah.

'Don't try to be clever. You checked it earlier. Now move!' He shoved her forward into the snow. Keeler followed, carrying the precious container.

The trio rounded the corner of the farthest hut and set off across the open waste. It was still snowing, but the first few streaks of dawn were beginning to lighten the sky. Sarah wondered briefly if she would live to see another day.

Inside the Crew Quarters the Doctor had wriggled to his feet and was hopping up and down like a jack-in-a box. Above his head hung an old hurricane lamp for use in emergencies. Stevenson observed the Doctor's antics in puzzlement.

'What are you doing?'

'Ever played football?' gasped the Doctor, as he headed the lamp off its hook and on to the floor. The glass smashed into fragments. 'Quick!'

Stevenson inched over to the Doctor whose fingers had grabbed a piece of the broken glass. 'Now keep very still, or I might cut a blood vessel.' The Doctor began to saw away at the rope around Stevenson's wrists.

Outside, in the cold dawn, the creature observed the lights of the Camp from behind a hillock of snow. It was now seven or eight feet high. After a moment or two, it set off towards the Camp, moving at exceptional speed, its long fibrous tentacles dragging behind in the snow. It reached the nearest hut and began to edge slowly along the side looking for a way in.

The trek across the snowy waste seemed to Sarah like a march to the guillotine, an inexorable journey to certain death. Once inside the Power Unit, Scorby tied her to a heavy pipe on the wall and then started to fix an explosive device to the side of the Fuel Cell.

'This bomb will set off a fault in the system which in turn will blow up the entire Camp, leaving no clues whatsoever. Ingenious, don't you think?'

'You're twisted ... evil!' replied Sarah. 'Why kill us all? Why not just take the pod?'

Scorby leered sadistically. 'You know too much.' He finished wiring the charge and picked up the pod container. 'Come on, Keeler, let's get airborne.'

Sarah suddenly noticed Keeler's strange, tortured expression. 'No ... no ... I can't let you do this!' He lunged at Scorby. 'It's cold-blooded murder!'

Scorby brushed him aside. 'Too late,' he snarled. 'I've already started the count-down.' He turned to Sarah. 'You won't have long to wait. Ten minutes at the most.' He strode out. Keeler shot Sarah a final, anguished look, then hurried after.

The door slammed shut and Sarah heard the bolt drawn across. She glanced at the detonator. The numerals on the clock were clearly visible. They read five hundred and eighty seconds. She struggled to free her bonds but knew it was hopeless.

With a final wrench the Doctor released his wrists from the biting rope and headed for the door. 'I'll get after the pod ... and Sarah,' he snapped at Stevenson. 'You contact Main Base on the radio and see if they can intercept the aircraft.'

'What about the Krynoid?'

'We'll have to take a chance on that,' cried the Doctor and dashed out. Stevenson hobbled after him into the corridor, rubbing his wrists and ankles.

The Doctor set out from the Camp at a run, his eyes scanning the murky grey landscape. 'Sarah! Sarah!' His voice died on the wind. Although it was nearly daylight the snowfall was still heavy. He hesitated a moment then headed in the direction of the landing strip. They had probably made straight for the plane. It was a slim chance, but he might still be able to stop them taking off.

In the Lab, Stevenson was feverishly plugging up the radio. 'Hello Main Base ... hello Main Base ... can you hear me? ... Over.' The line seemed dead. 'Hello Main Base? Over.' Nothing.

Behind him the door began to open slowly and a fibrous tentacle pushed its way into the room.

'Hello ... this is Camp Three calling Main Base. Can you hear me ... can you hear me?' He threw down the headphones and inspected the back of the equipment. Immediately he saw the damage.

'Sabotage!' he whispered to himself. Then suddenly he realised he was not alone. He whirled round. A terrifying mass of green tentacles was bearing down on him.

'No ... no ...!' Stevenson stumbled back, crashing

46

into the radio. But there was no escape. The tentacles were all round him and closing in. He let out a last desperate cry as the Krynoid enveloped him totally.

In the Power Unit, Sarah stared mesmerised as the seconds ticked away.

The Doctor pounded through the snow, his scarf flailing in the wind. What a fool he had been. The pod stolen by a thug with a gun! The consequences were incalculable.

All at once a fresh noise cut through the howl of the wind. The Doctor stopped and strained his ears. It was a plane taking off. He was too late. The thought stabbed him like a knife. Sarah? He hardly dared contemplate her fate. He turned back towards the Camp, a lonely and dejected figure. His gaze swept the glaring white snowscape but took nothing in.

Then, abruptly, he jerked to life again. Looming out of the snow a few hundred yards away was the dark shape of the Power Unit building. He set off towards it at full pelt.

Not far away, but hidden by the ridge, another figure also moved quickly through the snow. But this figure was not human, and its purpose was deadly.

Click ... click ... click ... The dial showed less than a minute to go. Sarah felt the panic rise inside her as the ropes refused to give. Suddenly she heard a scrabbling outside the door. Her heart missed a beat. Then it was flung open and the Doctor burst in. With one bound he was by her side and untying the ropes.

'Doctor! The whole Camp is going to be blown sky high any second!' Expertly the Doctor unravelled Sarah's knots and took in the bomb with a hurried glance. There was no time to defuse it.

Sarah pulled one arm free. 'Where's Stevenson?'

'I'll have to try and save him.' The Doctor released her other arm and hauled Sarah to her feet. 'Come on!'

Sarah took one pace then froze. 'Doctor, *look!*' She pointed to the door. The Doctor spun round. Blocking the doorway was the monstrous bulk of the Krynoid. From its body sprouted a hundred tentacles, each as thick as a man's arm. Where once a face had existed there was now a gnarled and twisted mass of bark. It remained in the doorway, swaying from side to side and emitting a low, unearthly rattle.

'Get behind me,' whispered the Doctor. Sarah did so. She could hear the bomb ticking quite clearly.

The Krynoid started to advance. The Doctor edged round the wall. Suddenly the creature rushed towards them. The Doctor side-stepped, pulling Sarah with him, and one of the green tentacles caught on the metal grid protecting the Fuel Cell. There was a flash and the Krynoid roared in pain.

'Run!' yelled the Doctor and bundled Sarah towards

the door. As she passed the creature Sarah felt a cold, slimy tentacle brush her face. She let out a scream and the next thing she knew she was pitched into the wet snow. Behind her, the Doctor slammed the door and slid the bolt into position.

'Get away!' he shouted and raced off in the direction of the Camp. With horror Sarah realised he still hoped to rescue Stevenson.

'There isn't time!' she cried, but the Doctor was already out of earshot. Sarah glanced again at the Power Unit. It was about to explode. She sprinted for the cover of the ridge.

Inside, the Krynoid pounded the door in a frenzy. EIGHT ... SEVEN ... SIX ... It managed to prise one tentacle through ... FIVE ... FOUR ...

Sarah could see the ridge. Only a few yards further. THREE ... TWO ...

The Doctor came in sight of the Camp. He opened his mouth to yell. 'Stev ...' There was a searing flash of red, the ground shook, a firework seemed to explode in his head. Then he was sinking ... sinking ... sinking into a white cloud of nothingness ...

5

Betrayal

Sarah woke. She found herself staring up at a clear blue sky. She tried to sit up but there was no sensation in her arms or legs. For one awful moment she wondered if she had lost them. Then she realised they were numb with cold.

Suddenly a foot crunched in the snow a few inches from her head. A muffled figure in furs and goggles loomed over her.

'I almost missed you in the snow,' it said in a familiar English accent.

Sarah smiled weakly. 'Yes, well, there's rather a lot of it about.'

'Are you all right?'

'I think so.'

The man helped her to her feet. 'We're from South Bend. Medical Team. We heard the explosion. What happened?'

The explosion! It came back with a rush. The Doctor! Where was he? She began to run towards the Camp like a mad thing. More figures jumped from a Snocat in pursuit. Panting, Sarah reached the top of the ridge only to let out a gasp of horror. Where once the Camp had stood, there was now only a heap of blackened ash and twisted metal. A few wisps of smoke curled up into the blue sky. She looked back at the

Power Unit. That too had completely disappeared.

Stunned, Sarah lowered her gaze. As she did so she gave a cry of fear. Sticking out of the snow a few feet away was a hand.

'Doctor!' she screamed, and began to claw frantically at the snow. Moments later strong arms arrived and pulled the inert figure of the Doctor from the snow. Desperately Sarah slapped his face to try and revive him. 'Doctor! Wake up! *Wake Up!*'

For a while nothing happened. Then slowly one eye opened and winked. The grin she knew so well spread across the Doctor's face and he spoke. 'Good morning.'

Sarah breathed a sigh of relief and smiled back. She was never more grateful in her life to hear those two simple words.

Harrison Chase sat in his library glowing with triumph. On the desk in front of him stood the thermocontainer.

'Well open it! Open it!' he ordered. Keeler removed the lid to reveal the pod. Chase stared at it with greedy fascination.

'I must hold it,' he whispered and lovingly lifted out the strange, green object.

'It's all right in its present state,' advised Keeler, 'but we must be careful.'

'Why?'

'The other pod infected one of their men.'

Chase abruptly replaced the pod. 'Infected? What happened?'

Keeler explained.

'Incredible!' said Chase. 'You're sure the other one was destroyed?'

'The whole scientific base, and everybody in it, was obliterated,' said Scorby smugly.

'Excellent. Regrettable, but excellent.' Chase gazed at the pod once more. 'Think of it, gentlemen,' he said. 'If the theory is correct, this has come to us across thousands of years and millions of miles.'

'The last few miles caused a bit of trouble,' muttered Scorby.

'Trouble?' scoffed Chase. 'Nothing would be too much trouble for *this*!' The intercom buzzed on his desk. 'Yes, Hargreaves?'

'Mr Dunbar of WEB is here to see you, sir.'

'Send him in.' Chase clicked off the receiver.

A moment later, a distraught looking Dunbar was ushered in. He hesitated at the sight of Keeler and Scorby.

'It's all right,' explained Chase smoothly. 'These are the two men who brought back the pod.'

Dunbar spoke with suppressed fury. 'I had no idea you would go to such terrible lengths to get it!'

'The destruction of the others was necessary.' Chase spoke without emotion.

'Necessary!' repeated Dunbar, appalled.

'You've been handsomely rewarded for your part, Dunbar, so put on a stiff upper lip and forget your qualms. The object has been achieved.' Chase gestured towards the pod. 'We can all relax.'

Dunbar took a pace forward. 'Not quite.'

Chase stiffened. 'What do you mean?'

'They weren't all wiped out. That's what I came to warn you about. The Doctor and his assistant are still alive.'

'Impossible!' hissed Chase.

'The Doctor is meeting us at WEB in an hour's time.' Dunbar waited for the effect of his news.

Keeler and Scorby shifted uneasily on the spot. Chase turned to face them, his eyes blazing. 'You asinine bunglers!'

'You were very lucky, Doctor.'

The speaker was Sir Colin Thackeray, Director of the World Ecology Bureau, a large distinguished-looking man with a rather precise manner.

'Simple presence of mind,' replied the Doctor dismissively.

'Are you quite certain it was sabotage?' Dunbar spoke now.

'That explosion was no accident,' said Sarah Jane firmly. She had recovered from the ordeal but appeared tired after the trip back to England.

Sir Colin looked puzzled. 'Why on earth should anyone want to possess a thing like that so badly?'

'Greed! The most dangerous impulse in the Galaxy,' exclaimed the Doctor, jumping to his feet and addressing them all. 'You realise that on this planet the pod is unique—I use the word with precision—and to some people its uniqueness makes it desirable at any cost.'

'You make these men sound like fanatics,' said Dunbar derisively.

The Doctor sauntered over to the side of the room and peered at a model of the Antarctic Base. 'No,' he said slowly, 'I think they were working for someone else.'

'The real fanatic,' added Sarah.

'What's more to the point is how they got on to it.' The Doctor spun round to face Dunbar. 'The expedition had only reported its discovery to this office, right?'

Dunbar coloured. 'Doctor, I trust you aren't suggesting information was leaked from this Bureau?'

'Yes, what would be the gain from it?' intervened Sir Colin.

'Money,' replied the Doctor sharply. 'Thieves and murderers don't usually work for love.'

'Since you seem to have this business sewn up, Doctor, where do you think the pod is now?' Dunbar sounded aggressive.

'I'd make a guess and say—right in this country.' The Doctor crossed to Sir Colin and jabbed him in the chest. 'Action, Sir Colin, that's what is needed. If we don't find that pod before it germinates, it will be the end of everything—even your pension!'

This last thought seemed to galvanise Sir Colin into

activity. 'Of course, Doctor, we'll do all we can to help. The entire facilities of this Bureau are at your disposal.' He glared at his Deputy, 'All right, Dunbar?'

Dunbar nodded. 'I'll organise anything you require.'

'Good,' snapped the Doctor. 'Then organise us to the Botanical Institute.'

A few minutes later the unmistakable figures of the Doctor and his assistant emerged from the entrance of the World Ecology Bureau. A uniformed chauffeur approached them. 'Doctor?'

'Yes.'

'This car was ordered for you, sir.' He indicated a large, black limousine.

'How kind. After you, Sarah.' They climbed in, the Doctor gave instructions to the chauffeur, and the car moved off.

Alone in his office, Dunbar dialled a number. Someone answered the other end. Dunbar leant closer into the phone and whispered, 'It's all right, they're being taken care of.'

'Excellent,' replied the voice and hung up. Dunbar replaced the receiver thoughtfully.

The limousine was approaching the outskirts of London. The Doctor had remained pensive and silent throughout the journey and Sarah had chosen not to disturb him. She looked out of the window as the car turned down a side road and into open country. The

Botanical Institute was farther out of town than she thought.

Suddenly the car lurched to a halt. The road had become little more than a dirt track leading to what seemed like a disused quarry. The Doctor jerked to life. 'What's going on?'

The chauffeur turned round, a revolver in his hand. 'We're in a nice deserted place, Doctor. Now—both of you—out!' He slipped from behind the wheel and, keeping them covered, opened the rear passenger door.

The Doctor winked. 'I think we'd better do as he says, Sarah.' He started to get out slowly. Then, in one explosive action he swung the door violently at the chauffeur, knocked him flying into the mud and dragged Sarah from the car.

'Run!' he yelled, and the two of them sprinted away down the rutted track. Winded, the chauffeur groped for his revolver, but before he could take aim the two figures disappeared down a gully. He staggered to his feet and set off in pursuit.

One quick glance was sufficient for the Doctor to take in the quarry. A large sandhopper with a raised platform lay to their right. He changed direction towards it, shouting instructions to Sarah as he did so.

A few moments later the panting gunman arrived beneath the hopper. His captives had vanished—into thin air! To his left was an old pile of gravel, enough for a hiding place. He crept towards it, finger on the trigger. Suddenly, there was a noise behind him. He spun round and fired.

Twenty feet above his head the Doctor crouched on the hopper platform, poised to leap. He could see Sarah plainly behind the gravel pile. She picked up a second pebble and threw it in the air. The chauffeur turned and fired again, then took a pace forward, bringing him directly below the Doctor.

The Doctor eyed the drop one more time, noted the position of the revolver and launched himself into space. Thud! The chauffeur crumpled like a rag doll as the Doctor's fifteen and a half stones slammed into him. Sarah dashed out from behind the mound. The Doctor picked himself up and was about to administer a straight left when he realised his dive had laid the gunman out cold.

'He isn't dead?' said Sarah fearfully.

'Unconscious. It seems news travels fast from the South Pole.'

The Doctor gathered up the revolver and hurled it out of sight. 'Let's search the car.'

They ran back.

Clearly the limousine did not belong to the World Ecology Bureau. But who did own it? There appeared to be no clues inside the car.

Sarah suddenly called the Doctor to the boot. She was holding up a framed painting of a flower. In the corner was a signature.

'Amelia Ducat,' read the Doctor, puzzled.

'An original as well,' exclaimed Sarah excitedly. 'Must be worth something.'

'You think so?'

Sarah eyed the Doctor with disdain. 'You mean to say you haven't heard of Amelia Ducat? She's one of the country's leading flower artists.'

The Doctor glanced in the direction of the sand-hopper. 'Hardly a passion for a gunman,' he said with a grin. 'Still, let's see if Miss Ducat can throw any light on the subject.'

He leapt into the driving seat and, scarcely allowing Sarah time to climb in, accelerated off towards the main road.

'Ah yes ... a perfect example of Fritillaria Meleagris.'

The speaker was an eccentric little lady in her sixties, dressed in heavy tweeds; a pair of gold-rimmed spectacles dangled on a chain round her neck and a large cigar jutted from the side of her mouth. She held the painting at arm's length admiringly. 'Rather good, don't you think?'

The Doctor smiled indulgently. 'We're trying to trace the owner, Miss Ducat.'

'You mean it isn't yours?'

'No. We found it in a car boot.'

'In a car boot?' Miss Ducat looked horrified. 'How insensitive!'

'So was the driver,' chipped in Sarah. 'He tried to kill us.'

'Good gracious! Whatever for?'

The Doctor leant over the top of Miss Ducat's easel,

which held a half-completed painting. 'Miss Ducat,' he said, in his friendliest and most coaxing tone, 'do you remember who bought this painting?'

Miss Ducat stared, a little puzzled, at the painting in front of her. 'Nobody. It isn't finished yet.'

'No, this one, Miss Ducat,' explained Sarah. 'Fritillaria Melewhatsit.'

'Ah ... oh ... let me see now ...' Miss Ducat took a couple of good puffs on her cigar and coughed violently 'It was six or seven years ago ...' She closed her eyes in deep concentration. 'Lace? ... Mace? ... Paice? ... Race? ...' Miss Ducat struggled manfully.

'Brace?' said Sarah.

'Grace?' tried the Doctor.

'Chase!' shouted Miss Ducat triumphantly. 'Harrison Chase the millionaire!' A strange look came over her. 'Good Lord,' she said. 'He never paid me!'

Sarah glanced at the Doctor who suppressed a smile. 'Give me his address, Miss Ducat,' he said, 'and I'll see what I can do.'

Twenty minutes later the large, black limousine was cruising effortlessly through the countryside, the Doctor at the wheel. He was dressed in the chauffeur's dark blue raincoat.

'I hope this works,' said Sarah doubtfully.

'A risk worth taking,' replied the Doctor seriously. 'We must find that pod.'

The road now ran alongside the high wall of an

estate, topped with barbed wire, and signs at intervals marked 'DANGER—KEEP OUT'.

The Doctor spotted the gateway ahead and pulled the car into the verge. 'Ready?' He smiled encouragingly at Sarah. She ducked down beneath the windscreen out of sight. The Doctor doffed the chauffeur's peaked cap, glanced appreciatively at himself in the mirror and eased the car forward.

The heavy wooden gates were at least twenty feet high and studded with metal bolts like a prison entrance. From the look of things Mr Harrison Chase was a gentleman who valued his privacy. He was also a gentleman with friends in high places. On past evidence, their little contretemps with the chauffeur would soon be reported, and before then the Doctor knew he had to somehow penetrate Chase's domain and retrieve the pod.

He swung the car in front of the gates and beeped the horn. A uniformed guard poked his head through a small door set in the right-hand gate. He glanced at the car, nodded, then disappeared inside. Seconds later the gates parted and the Doctor accelerated through. The guard stood back as the car swept past, hardly giving it a look, then shut the gates again. The Doctor breathed a sigh of relief. He had banked correctly on this being a routine procedure.

They were now in the grounds of a large and imposing manor house, glimpses of which the Doctor caught through thick greenery bordering the approach road. He slowed down, searching for a fork which would lead round to the back of the property. Sure enough there was one. He steered the big car expertly down a narrow drive and pulled to a halt beneath a clump of trees.

'So far so good,' he whispered, and tapped Sarah on the shoulder.

She straightened up from her hiding position. 'Ouch! I'm sure there are more comfortable ways of travelling.' She rubbed her back painfully.

'We'll leave the car here,' said the Doctor, ignoring her complaint. He switched off the ignition and slid gently out of the car. Sarah did likewise.

The nearest place of cover was a crumbling wall with a series of elegant arches set into it. The Doctor moved silently towards the wall, Sarah in tow. From there they could see the house clearly across a wild expanse of overgrown lawn.

It was a magnificent Elizabethan manor house, large and rambling, with several courtyards and outbuildings running off it. The gardens immediately surrounding the house were a blaze of colour, a breathtaking profusion of flowers of every kind, but further from the house the vegetation grew thicker and more exotic, forming a jungle-like screen around the whole property.

'Lovely house,' whispered Sarah. 'What's the best way in?'

'Not the front door, I'm afraid.'

At that moment two uniformed guards appeared. They were no more than fifty yards away. Over their shoulders they carried vicious looking sten guns. It was obvious their course would bring them straight to where the Doctor and Sarah were hiding.

'We'll have to bluff it,' whispered the Doctor and stepped nonchalantly out into the open. Sarah's heart skipped a beat as she followed suit. Any second she expected to be enveloped in a hail of bullets. At the same time she found herself laughing inwardly at the comical figure of the Doctor, in the chauffeur's hat and coat, attempting to walk quickly yet casually away from the guards.

They were half way towards the house when a voice rang out behind them. 'Hey you!' The Doctor quickened his pace. 'Halt!' The sound of a safety catch being released was clearly audible.

'Run!' yelled the Doctor and sprinted towards a narrow gate at the side of the house.

'I said halt!'

The Doctor burst open the gate with his shoulder and pushed Sarah through. As he did so a shower of bullets slammed into the masonry inches above his head and alarm bells began to ring inside the house.

They were now running along a narrow terrace. Suddenly, more guards appeared at the far end. The Doctor grabbed Sarah's arm and leapt with her off the terrace on to the ground and headed on a zig-zag course towards the surrounding cover of trees. The barking of tracker dogs could be heard above the din of bells and machine-gun fire. 'One thing is certain,' thought the Doctor, 'Harrison Chase doesn't take kindly to strangers.'

Seconds later they reached the belt of trees and plunged in. Branches, thorns and razor-sharp leaves cut their skin and clawed at their clothing as they crashed through the jungle-like vegetation.

'This way, Sarah,' gasped the Doctor and struck out to his left. The hue and cry was falling behind them and to their right. Any plan to penetrate the house was now useless, but if they could make the outer wall, thought the Doctor, they might still escape. Ahead of them appeared a solid mass of giant bamboo. Sarah felt she was acting out a nightmare. This couldn't be happening in England. The Doctor beat a way through. 'Come on, nearly there!' Sarah willed herself on.

Suddenly, she literally fell into a clearing. Ahead was a small pathway. The Doctor saw her fall and ran back. 'Quick!' He hauled her to her feet and dragged her forwards again. The blood was pounding through her veins and her lungs were bursting for air. Then, all at once, Sarah felt the Doctor's grip slacken. He had stopped.

'Hello, Doctor, I heard you were on your way.' Sarah froze as the unmistakable voice of Scorby cut through the air. Gun in hand, his familiar dark figure blocked the pathway ahead. At the same moment three armed guards appeared from nowhere and seized them both.

Scorby stepped up to them, savouring the moment. 'You weren't thinking of leaving, I hope. Mr Chase is so looking forward to meeting you.'

6

A Visit to Harrison Chase

Moments later the Doctor and Sarah found themselves inside the house. They were bundled along dark corridors and through a doorway into a large baronial hall. An oak-beamed ceiling towered above their heads, and on either side the panelled walls were lined with suits of armour and ancient hanging tapestries.

At the far end, seated in a throne-like chair, sat an immaculately dressed man wearing black gloves. Not for the first time in his life the Doctor sensed he was in the presence of danger and evil.

The figure rose as the two captives were pushed forward. 'So, the meddling Doctor.' The Doctor felt the man's powerful gaze sweep over him. 'You lead a charmed life. Not even a touch of frostbite.'

The Doctor eyed his opponent with undisguised contempt. 'Are you behind this whole murderous exercise?'

Ignoring the Doctor's challenge the man turned to Sarah. 'And Miss Smith—still beautifully intact, I see.' He leered at her.

'No thanks to your friend over there,' retorted Sarah, indicating Scorby.

'Hand over the pod, Chase,' commanded the Doctor

in a voice of steel. 'You're tampering with things you don't understand.'

Chase gave a chuckle. 'Hand it over? After all the trouble I've taken to acquire it? No, Doctor. My pod, when it finally flowers, will be the crowning glory of a life's work.' The voice grew shrill and excited. 'Perhaps you didn't know, Doctor, that I have assembled in this house the greatest collection of rare plants in the world.'

'Yes, I've noticed a bit of greenfly here and there.'

Chase's expression turned sour. 'Your envy, Doctor, is understandable. However, since I propose to have you both executed ...'

Sarah gasped incredulously. 'You're not going to kill us?'

'My dear Miss Smith, you leave me no option.' The voice regained its smooth, feline purr. 'You and the Doctor keep interfering ... As I was saying, however, you will be granted a unique privilege before you die.'

'How generous,' remarked the Doctor with heavy sarcasm.

Chase smiled coldly. 'The last thing you will ever see will be my beautiful collection of plants. Come this way.' He crossed to a side door.

'I've heard of flower power but this is ridiculous,' muttered Sarah under her breath.

A dig in the ribs from Scorby's gun put an end to further conversation, and she and the Doctor were propelled out of the room.

They were led to another part of the house, into what

looked like a large laboratory. Various experiments seemed to be in progress, supervised by white-coated technicians. Plants were being nourished by drips, like hospital patients, or supported on strange metal structures suspended from the ceiling. Chase ushered them in with mock politeness and pointed to a flower the Doctor had never seen before. 'This is the famous Shanghai Saffron. It ... er ... defected from the East last spring.'

The Doctor remained unimpressed. 'Are we going much further?' he said. 'I do so hate guided tours.'

Chase moved on, unheeding. 'Here we treat our green friends as patients. If they are puny, we build them up; if they are sick, we give them succour.' He paused by a row of plants which faced a battery of flashing blue bulbs.

'These must feel they're in a disco,' quipped Sarah.

Chase smiled. 'You've heard of the theory that irregular light patterns can effect the senses of so-called mindless things?'

The Doctor nodded. 'Yes, like Scorby here. Incidentally, where's his friend?'

'Keeler is engaged in important isolated research.'

'On the pod?'

'But of course.'

They continued towards a pair of large metallic doors, engraved with swirling designs in the shape of flowers. Chase swung them open with a flourish.

The sight which met their eyes made Sarah gasp with astonishment and even the Doctor raised an eye-

66

brow in surprise. Before them lay a vast expanse of luxuriant foliage. It spread out in all directions so that it was impossible to tell where the forest of green ended and the walls and ceiling began. As his two prisoners eyed the vivid tangle of plants and creepers, Chase strode to a gleaming metal box set into the stone wall and fiddled with some knobs. Immediately the air was filled with an eerie, discordant sound.

'The song of the plants,' cried Chase. 'I composed it myself. People say you should talk to plants. I believe that, just as I believe they also like music.'

'Doctor, we must get out of here,' whispered Sarah in desperation.

'Yes, the music is terrible.' The Doctor grinned at her. Sarah grimaced. This was no time for jokes. She scanned the room for possible exits, but apart from a long iron cat-walk which led into the thick of the creepers, there was nothing.

Suddenly an agitated figure, obviously the butler, burst into the room behind them. 'Mr Chase!' he called.

The music stopped abruptly. 'What is it, Hargreaves?'

'It's Mr Keeler—something is happening to that thing, sir. He wants you to go to the Special Projects room straight away.'

Chase turned to Scorby. 'Take them out,' he pointed at the Doctor and Sarah. 'I'll join you in a moment. I'm sure our two friends won't mind a slight delay before they die.' He swept towards the door.

The Doctor shouted after him. 'You're insane, Chase! You don't know what a terrible thing you are unleashing!'

Chase gave a sinister smile, but said nothing. An instant later he was gone.

Scorby immediately took command. He dismissed the remaining guards, then propelled the Doctor and Sarah out of the room at gunpoint. As they passed through seemingly endless stone corridors, the Doctor reflected dismally on their plight. They had fallen into the clutches of a madman—without doubt—and despite warnings, he was evidently conducting his own experiments on the pod. It was imperative to get to the pod and prevent any further risk. But how? They were being led to their deaths this very instant.

By now they had left the house and were being marched through the overgrown gardens. 'Where are you taking us, Scorby?' asked the Doctor.

'Don't worry, it's strictly a one-way journey,' came the chilling reply.

Ahead lay the same arched wall which had concealed them less than an hour beforehand. Imperceptibly the Doctor quickened his pace. Sarah was a fraction behind and a little to his right. Scorby followed, covering them with his gun.

As he drew level with the nearest arch the Doctor took a sudden step to his left, thus putting solid masonry between himself and the gun. Taken unawares Scorby let out a cry and raised his arm to fire. But the fleeting figure of the Doctor dodged about the arches without presenting a clear target. In the split second that Scorby's attention was diverted, Sarah seized her chance and leapt on his arm like a tigress. As Scorby struggled to shake himself free the Doctor darted in and sent the gun flying with a skilled, mule-like kick. Scorby wrenched himself clear of Sarah and lunged at the Doctor. The Doctor side-stepped, grabbed his head in a Venusian neck lock, and gave it a short, sharp twist. There was a nasty click and Scorby sank to the ground.

'Time to leave,' said the Doctor calmly, but Sarah needed no bidding this time, and the two of them hared off towards the undergrowth.

Once they had gained cover the Doctor paused. 'We can't handle this on our own,' he said. 'Sir Colin must be warned about the danger.'

'Right, so let's get out and phone him,' responded Sarah urgently.

'*You* are going to phone him,' ordered the Doctor. 'I'm staying here.'

Sarah began to argue but the Doctor cut her off. 'I must get a look at that pod ... see what state it's in.' He tore off the chauffeur's clothes. 'Come on, the outer wall can't be far.'

Pistol shots could now be heard and the distant barking of guard dogs. The Doctor led Sarah stealthily through the undergrowth like an Indian brave until, finally, they reached the high wall which skirted the perimeter of the grounds. Luckily the barbed wire had come away in places and there was just enough room for Sarah to squeeze through.

'Fancy a little mountaineering?' said the Doctor and hoisted Sarah on to his shoulders. The gun shots and barking were growing nearer. With difficulty, Sarah heaved herself to the top of the wall. There was a fifteen-foot drop on the other side.

'All right?' whispered the Doctor.

'I think so.' She took a deep breath and let go.

The Doctor heard her land heavily. 'The main road should be straight ahead. Good luck.'

'And to you.'

The Doctor waited until he was sure Sarah was on her way, then quickly retraced his steps towards the house.

Sarah pressed on towards the main road. She could hear the odd car passing and this kept her on a straight course. Although she was out of the grounds there was still a large stretch of woodland between herself and safety.

Suddenly, she froze like a statue. A twig had snapped near by. In front of her was a dense thicket. She scanned every branch and leaf for sign of movement. There was another, fluttering sound, then a blackbird flew out of a bush. Sarah let go her breath with relief and continued forward.

The next thing she knew a large hairy hand was clamped over her mouth and a voice from behind said, 'Make a sound, little girl, and you're dead.'

*

In the Special Projects room Chase was crouched inches away from the pod, as if in a trance. 'It's growing! It's alive!' he murmured, his eyes wide with rapture.

'I shouldn't get too close,' warned Keeler. 'From what happened at the Camp base, the germination could be spontaneous. It's alien, don't forget.'

Chase continued to stare spellbound at the pod. It was larger now, more bloated looking, and several cracks had begun to appear on the surface.

Suddenly Chase snapped out of his reverie. 'Inject more fixed nitrogen!' he ordered.

Keeler hesitated. 'I don't think that would be wise.'

Chase glared at him. 'I pay you, Keeler, so that *I* can make the decisions. Now, inject another fifteen grammes!'

Keeler nodded nervously and carried out the order.

The Doctor halted and peered through a clump of bushes towards the house. So far so good. He had performed a detour and calculated correctly that it would bring him out at the rear of the building. Apart from one guard posted on a corner he had a free run to some stone steps leading down to a basement door. Once in the house he then had to find the Special Projects room. He had a hunch it might be on the top floor where there would be plenty of light and more privacy.

He waited. The guard was still facing towards him.

After a few moments the guard took out a walkie-talkie receiver and put it to his ear. From his reaction the Doctor guessed he was receiving orders, perhaps news of their escape. The guard pocketed the receiver, took a quick glance round then ran off down the side of the house. The Doctor seized his opportunity and belted towards the steps. The door opened easily and he entered.

He was in a long, dark passage with a flag-stone floor. At the far end was a narrow staircase, originally for the servants' use, but probably still a good route to the top of the house. Cautiously, he traversed the passage and started up the stairs.

'I don't like it. It's like waiting for a bomb to explode.' Keeler rubbed his hands together in agitation and paced the room.

'Where's your enthusiasm, Keeler?' crowed Chase gleefully. 'This promises to be the high point of your career—a moment of history!'

Chase's triumphant mood was abruptly shattered as Scorby burst in, dragging Sarah behind him.

'I thought you had them safely locked up?' he hissed.

'They escaped,' replied Scorby sheepishly. 'A guard found this one in the woods beyond the wall. The Doctor's still at large.'

Chase crossed to Sarah and grabbed her savagely beneath the chin. 'Where is he?' he demanded.

Sarah stared defiantly back at him. 'I don't know, and if I did I wouldn't tell you.'

'How uncooperative. However, I've just had an idea. You're going to help with my experiment. Remove her coat.'

Scorby quickly tore Sarah's coat from her shoulders. 'What are we going to do, boss?'

Chase dragged Sarah over to the bench. 'Miss Smith will be our subject ... like so. Get some clamps!' He forced Sarah's arm on to the bench. Sarah let out a gasp of horror as she caught sight of the pod.

'You can't! It's inhuman!' protested Keeler.

'I don't care,' cried Chase. 'I must see what happens when the Krynoid touches human flesh!'

Sarah struggled desperately as they clamped her arm to the bench. Already the pod was beginning to throb and split in places. Chase stood gloating at the sight, like a fiend possessed.

The Doctor reached the top of the stairs. It was dark and dusty, and there was very little headroom. Through the gloom he could just make out a door down a narrow passage. He clambered along and tried the knob. The door opened to reveal an attic with a second door which led on to the roof of the house. He crawled out. To his left was a large section made of glass. He edged towards it and peered through.

The sight which met him made his blood run cold. Twenty feet below in the room, Sarah was imprisoned in a chair, with one arm clamped to a wooden bench. Less than twelve inches away lay the pod, hideously swollen and vibrating menacingly. Even as the Doctor looked it began to break open.

7

Condemned to Die

The Doctor launched himself through the glass roof in a spectacular dive, landing feet first on the bench. It snapped instantly beneath his weight, spewing plants, instruments and broken glass in all directions. Before anyone had time to react, the Doctor hurled Scorby to the ground, grabbed his gun and yanked Sarah clear of the pod.

'Untie her!' he yelled fiercely. Keeler started to release Sarah.

Chase, his hands held high, watched in cool amusement. 'What do you do for an encore, Doctor?' he asked.

The Doctor levelled the gun at Chase. 'I win,' he smiled. 'Come on, Sarah.'

Sarah followed the Doctor to the door. He pushed her outside, followed then quickly slammed the door and locked it behind them.

Chase ran across the room and hammered on the door in impotent fury. 'Guards! Guards!'

Stunned by the force of the Doctor's throw, Scorby stirred and groaned feebly. Chase continued to pound the door.

Suddenly, a blood-curdling scream rent the air. 'Aaarrgh! . . . my arm . . . my arm . . .'

Chase spun round. In the midst of the confusion the pod had burst, and now a long green tendril was digging into the flesh of Keeler's right arm. A look of horrified fascination came over Chase as Keeler began to stagger around the room in agony. An instant later, the door was thrown open and a mob of guards rushed in.

'Quick! Get after the Doctor and that girl,' ordered Chase. 'They must not escape!'

The guards charged off. Chase went back to Keeler. Already a terrifying change was taking place. Keeler's face and arms were turning a strange, mottled green.

'Do something ...' he pleaded, overcome with shock and fear.

Chase watched in icy detachment. 'Amazing ... absolutely unique!'

'What's happening?' Scorby came round muzzily, then let out a cry of disbelief as he focused on Keeler.

'Slept well, did you?' snarled Chase. 'Now get out and find that Doctor.' Scorby picked himself off the floor and hurried out. 'And be careful, he's got your gun!' Chase yelled after him. He turned to Keeler. 'We've got to get over to the cottage, where we can look after you properly.'

There was something in the way Chase said this which made Keeler's blood run cold, but before he had time to protest he was being manhandled out of the room by his master and the ever present Hargreaves.

*

After escaping, the Doctor led Sarah down the rear stairs and out of the house. He had noticed earlier a small shed set against a stone wall, used for storing garden equipment. He hurriedly guided Sarah towards it and thrust her in.

'Keep out of sight. I'll be back as soon as I can.'

'Where are you going?'

'To destroy the pod ... before it's too late.'

Sarah looked horrified. 'You can't tackle them single-handed.'

The Doctor flourished Scorby's pistol. 'I've got a gun.'

'You'd never use it.'

The Doctor grinned. 'True. But they don't know that.' He gave her a reassuring squeeze and crept off. Sarah climbed into her hidey hole, and settled down to wait.

Hidden by the thick foliage, the Doctor watched the rear of the building as a group of heavy-booted guards emerged and fanned out into the grounds. Then, when all was clear, he flitted across to the basement door and re-entered the house. Using the same route as before he quickly reached the entrance to the Special Projects room. The door was ajar and no sound came from within. Puzzled, the Doctor tiptoed in, gun at the ready.

The room was empty. With a pang of dismay the Doctor saw the pod had already burst open. He crossed the debris-strewn floor and, laying his gun aside, picked up a fragment of the pod to examine it.

'Rather stupid of you to return, Doctor,' said an unpleasant voice from the doorway.

The Doctor spun round to see Scorby covering him with a machine gun. 'I see I am too late. The pod has burst. I hope there was no one in the way.'

'Unfortunately there was. Our friend Keeler. Very clumsy of him.'

'Then we could all be doomed,' said the Doctor quietly.

'Don't exaggerate, Doctor,' snarled Scorby. 'Where's the girl?'

'Gone to get help,' lied the Doctor. Then, with vehemence, 'You're working for a madman, Scorby, you know that?'

'He pays well,' came the reply. 'And don't lie about Miss Smith. She'll never get out of this place ... alive.' He pocketed the pistol on the bench and motioned the Doctor out of the room.

The two of them marched quickly along a series of corridors and stairways towards the other end of the house.

'Not another guided tour, I hope,' quipped the Doctor.

'You'll soon see this is no time for joking,' replied Scorby, stopping at a grey, metal door. He opened it and pushed the Doctor in. 'Mr Chase has prepared a highly novel method for your execution.'

The Doctor descended a flight of stone steps and found himself in a large basement room filled with dustbins and refuse. At the far end stood a huge piece of machinery, covering one entire wall. It consisted of two enormous metal rollers with steel blades, like a giant lawn mower. The rollers were fed by a wide aluminium conveyor belt with vertical polished sides, about six feet deep. The Doctor guessed there must be a chute behind the rollers which led out through the wall and into the gardens.

The front of the conveyor belt was lowered at the moment, like a drawbridge, and a guard was busy emptying waste into it. The guard stopped work as they entered and, at Scorby's command, proceeded to bind the Doctor's arms and legs with a length of thick rope.

The Doctor eyed Scorby's machine gun and realised there was little point in resisting. He inspected his surroundings nonchalantly and sniffed the air. 'Isn't it about time you emptied the dustbins?'

'We will,' said Scorby. 'Soon,' and he gave a peculiar smile.

Sarah looked anxiously at her watch. The Doctor had been gone almost an hour. That could only mean one thing.

She peered out. Dusk had already fallen and it was probably dark enough to afford some cover. Sarah made her decision. She had to act now, either to escape and get help, or rescue the Doctor herself. *If* she could find him. She emerged warily from hiding and moved off.

Unknown to Sarah, but not far away, Chase and Hargreaves had dragged the infected Keeler to a cottage in the grounds. He now lay upstairs on a bed staring vacantly at the ceiling, while the butler pinioned his arms and legs with strong rope.

The activity seemed to shake him out of his stupor and he suddenly began to struggle. 'What are you doing?'

'It's for your own good,' said Chase.

'You can't keep me here. I need proper medical attention.' He tried to move an arm but fell back exhausted. His skin was rapidly changing into a vegetable texture and his limbs were beginning to lose their human shape.

'Remarkable,' said Chase excitedly. 'We must observe the process carefully.'

Keeler looked pleadingly at Hargreaves. 'Don't listen to him. This isn't an experiment—it's murder!'

'You're privileged, Keeler,' continued Chase enraptured. 'You're becoming a plant ... a marvellous new species of plant!'

He rose and beckoned Hargreaves to the door. 'Don't worry,' he whispered, 'everything will be all right, just so long as we keep him here.' He led the butler out of the bedroom and down the stairs.

Sarah hurried through the undergrowth. It was now dark and difficult to see. She suspected she was lost and a feeling of panic began to grip her.

Suddenly she came to a path. Voices sounded ahead and a flicker of light illuminated the grass. Straining her eyes she made out a small, thatched cottage. As she watched, the low wooden door opened and Chase and the butler stepped out. They walked briskly along the path towards her. Sarah darted back into the shadows. The two men brushed past without noticing her and disappeared into the gloom.

For a second she was tempted to follow, but intuition told her to investigate the cottage. It was just possible the Doctor had been taken there as prisoner. She crept forward and gently opened the door.

Inside, the cottage was dark, apart from a glimmer of candlelight overhead. Sarah groped her way to the foot of the stairs. All at once she heard a sound, a pitiful inhuman moan, which chilled her spine. Shaking, she mounted the steps. At the top stood a closed wooden door. She raised the latch and entered.

The sight in the room transfixed her with horror. A monstrous, hybrid creature lay on the bed, half human, half vegetable.

'You should be glad,' it croaked. 'This might have been you.'

Sarah could not speak as the hideous picture swam before her eyes.

'This must be how Winlett changed,' continued the voice. 'You saw him at the Base, didn't you?'

Sarah nodded.

'What was he like? You've got to tell me.'

Sarah forced herself to look at the grotesque shape

on the bed. It was true. The process was happening all over again. And she was powerless to stop it.

'Why are they keeping you here?' she managed to whisper finally.

'Chase ... Chase owns me, body and soul.'

'I must get to the Doctor,' said Sarah urgently.

A cunning expression appeared on the creature's face. 'Let me loose,' it breathed. 'We'll go together.' It strained at the ropes.

Sarah hesitated. She could no longer be sure. 'You aren't well enough,' she said, trying to conceal her fear.

'You're as bad as Chase and the others!' The voice became hard and rasping.

'That's not true.'

'... You want me to die!' The figure struggled to rise.

Alarmed, Sarah backed towards the door. As she did so she heard a noise from below. Someone was entering the cottage! She looked round frantically for somewhere to hide as heavy footsteps ascended the stairs.

8

The Krynoid Strikes

The footsteps halted outside the door. Just in time Sarah spied a large wardrobe standing in a corner. She snatched it open and dived in.

Through a narrow chink in the wardrobe she watched as the black-jacketed figure of Hargreaves entered the room. He carried a silver tray which he placed beside the bed. The creature had slumped back as if semi-conscious, and lay quietly groaning. On the tray were chunks of raw meat. The butler made sure the food was within reach of the creature's 'arm', then after checking the ropes were still secure, he left the room.

As soon as she heard the front door close, Sarah emerged from the wardrobe. She gave a final, horrified glance at the bed, and slipped quietly away.

Once out of the cottage Sarah tried to get her bearings. It was very dark, although a little pale moonlight filtered down through the trees, casting spooky shadows. Sarah shivered. It was only a matter of time now before the creature in the cottage became a second, deadly Krynoid. The Doctor had to be warned, always supposing he was still alive. Sarah quickly banished that awful thought from her mind and set off through the trees. If the Doctor was captive he must be in the house, and the house could not be far away because Hargreaves had returned so soon with the food.

She followed a narrow winding footpath which crossed a stream by a small footbridge. Sure enough there was the main house, about two hundred yards beyond. One or two lights shone out on to the surrounding gardens and she could see uniformed guards patrolling the ground floor.

Soundlessly, Sarah tiptoed across the thick grass and gained the cover of the outside wall. Then she worked her way methodically round the house until she came to some steps leading down to a basement door. Without knowing it, she had stumbled on the same entrance as the Doctor. She slid into the dark stone corridor and made her way stealthily towards the interior of the house.

The Doctor glanced uneasily at the crushing machine for the umpteenth time. He was now in no doubt about his imminent execution or the manner in which it would take place. Every ten minutes he had been privileged to witness the giant rollers of the machine devour several tons of garbage in no uncertain fashion. It was clear that the addition of one extra, live body would not cause the slightest hiccup in the functioning of this engineering masterpiece.

These morbid reflections were brought to an abrupt halt as the ever watchful guard sprang to attention. A moment later Harrison Chase entered.

He smiled grimly at the Doctor. 'You've seen my little toy?'

'Most efficient,' demurred the Doctor.

'The problem is keeping it stocked up.' Chase gestured towards the empty bins.

'Yes. At the moment it's working on an empty stomach,' joked the Doctor wryly. As if to emphasise this point the machine shuddered to a stop.

Chase crossed to the wall and reset the timer. 'The next time,' he purred, 'we must give it something to chew on.' He looked meaningfully at the Doctor. 'You may have noticed how lush the grounds are. This is the secret.' He patted the side of the crusher affectionately. 'We use everything in the grinder ... every scrap of food and gardening waste ... lots of other things too ... provided they are organic.'

The Doctor at that moment felt decidedly organic. 'What's happening to Keeler?' he asked, changing the subject.

'None of us can help Keeler now,' came the smooth reply, 'but properly nurtured he can be of inestimable value to science.'

With a shock the Doctor realised Keeler had become another of Chase's experiments. Was there no end to this man's devilry? He fixed Chase with an iron stare. 'Don't you understand what you are breeding?'

'A plant, Doctor, a human plant. And nothing is going to stop me.' Chase motioned to the guard who prodded the Doctor on to the aluminium conveyor belt and closed off the access door. Hands and feet tied, he was now crouched in the belly of the crusher, the vertical metal sides giving him no hope of escape and effectively screening out his vision. In front, a few feet away, hung the lethal steel blades, motionless for the time being.

He heard Chase turn a switch on the wall. 'Your death, Doctor, will be agonising, but mercifully quick.'

'How considerate.'

'After shredding,' intoned Chase's voice, 'your remains will pass automatically through my Compost Acceleration Chamber, and within ten minutes you will be pumped into the garden to become part of nature's grand design.'

'But the Krynoid isn't part of that design, Chase,' retorted the Doctor. 'Once its growth starts, you'll never manage to contain it. Nobody will be safe!'

Chase let out a loud cackle. 'You underestimate me, Doctor. Now say your prayers. You have only a few minutes left.' The hideous laugh rang out again. Then the door was slammed shut and everything went quiet, except for the faint ticking of the automatic time switch.

On the main road a few hundred yards from the entrance to Chase's estate a dark grey Rover three litre was parked surreptitiously under the trees, its lights doused. Inside sat Sir Colin Thackeray and Dunbar.

'I don't like it,' said Sir Colin grimly. 'I don't like it

at all.' He drummed his fingers on the steering wheel.

Dunbar remained silent. He seemed distracted, as if wrestling with something inside himself.

'I'm going to call in the Doctor's friends at UNIT,' snapped Sir Colin finally. 'This is getting too big for us.'

'No, wait!' interrupted Dunbar. 'Let me go in alone.'

'You'll never get past the gate.'

'Yes I will,' replied Dunbar quietly.

'What?'

'I've made a terrible mistake, Sir Colin. It's my duty now to try and save the situation.'

Before Sir Colin could stop him, Dunbar sprang out of the car. 'Give me half an hour. If I'm not back by then, return to London and contact UNIT.' He slammed the car door shut and hurried off into the darkness.

Sarah paused. The house was a rabbit-warren of corridors and passageways, any one of which could lead straight into the arms of the guards. Her progress so far had been slow and cautious.

Suddenly she heard a strange noise—a kind of grinding and thumping. It seemed to be coming from under the floor! She looked around. There was a small door at the far end of the passage. She opened it and found a flight of stone steps leading down to a lower level. The noise grew louder. She crept along this underground passage until she was directly beneath the spot where she had first heard the sound. A heavy metal door, not immediately visible, was recessed into the stone wall. The thumping noise came from inside.

Swiftly, Sarah heaved the door open. Straightaway her ears were split by a deafening blast of sound, as if huge strips of metal were being ripped apart and pounded into pieces. This thunderous screeching emanated from a mass of moving machinery at the far end of the room. Two enormous rollers were rising and falling in unison, slowly grinding together as they did so like a pair of giant molars. In front, a shiny aluminium conveyor belt was chugging inexorably towards this gaping maw. In it lay the Doctor!

Sarah flew across the room. 'Doctor!'

'Quick, Sarah, the switch!' he yelled above the din. His head was only inches from the murderous whirling blades.

Desperately Sarah scanned the wall. There were several levers. She pulled one. The noise increased and the machinery began to accelerate.

'The other one!' cried the Doctor.

Sarah yanked a second lever. Nothing happened. The Doctor was flattened against the sides of the conveyor. The rollers reared up again and began to descend towards him. In a mad flurry Sarah pulled all the levers she could find. Suddenly the noise subsided, the rollers ceased their descent, and came to rest a hair's breadth from the Doctor's face. Sarah let out a sob of relief and ran to release him. The Doctor looked up and gave her a charming smile.

'I believe that's what's known as a close shave,' he said.

Pale and tense, Dunbar confronted Chase across the wide baronial hall.

'Abandon the experiment? My dear Dunbar, nothing will stop me now. This is the most valuable study in plant biology ever made.' The ghost of a smile flickered over his cat-like features.

Suddenly a distraught-looking Hargreaves rushed in.

'What is it?' snapped Chase, annoyed by this unusual interruption.

'That thing in the cottage ... it's breaking loose!'

Chase's jaw dropped. 'It can't be ...'

'The ropes, sir. They're not going to hold it!'

'You mean that monster could be roaming around?' cut in Dunbar.

'I'm afraid so, sir.'

Dunbar's eyes widened in alarm at the thought.

All at once, there was a scuffle of footsteps and Scorby burst into the room. 'The Doctor's escaped!'

'He seems to be making a habit of it!' said Chase, his face contorting into a paroxysm of rage.

Dunbar took a pace forward and gripped the desk. 'You're mad, Chase! Raving mad!' He was beginning to sweat.

'There's no need to panic, Dunbar.'

'I'm going to get help. If this thing is free it could kill us all!' He started to back towards the door.

Chase's voice, icy cold, stabbed the air. 'I would prefer it if nobody else was told of this, Dunbar.'

'No. It's all gone far enough. I'm getting out of here and no one's going to stop me.' Dunbar suddenly drew a gun and brandished it hysterically.

'You won't make it past the guards,' said Chase coolly.

Dunbar reached the open doorway. 'We'll see.'

Scorby reached for his own gun but before he could use it Dunbar let off a shot. The men in the room ducked instinctively, giving Dunbar time to slam the door and belt off down the corridor.

While this was happening Sarah had swiftly and expertly guided the Doctor back to the cottage. Now, as they approached the low thatched building, Sarah started to tremble. The Doctor drew closer and gave her hand a reassuring squeeze.

They entered and climbed the stairs. Everything was ominously quiet. The Doctor carefully eased open the bedroom door and peered in.

The bed was empty. The ropes lay shattered, burst like string by a superhuman force.

'Where's it gone?' whispered Sarah.

The Doctor gave her a grim look. There was only one place the Krynoid could be; lurking in the blackness outside, just as its predecessor had prowled the snowy wastes several days before.

There was no time to lose! The Doctor leapt down the rickety wooden steps, grabbed a rusty sword from above the fireplace and dashed out into the night with Sarah in tow.

Dunbar moved through the woods, pistol at the ready. The most he had gained was a minute's start. Scorby and the guards, with machine guns and dogs, were already tracking him down. Escape through the main gate was impossible. He had to give them the slip in the woods and somehow make it over the wall.

As he struggled through the creepers and bushes Dunbar cursed his own weakness. Greed, that ancient vice of man, had ensnared him into a lurid web of murder and betrayal. Now, in this tangled wilderness, which plucked his clothes and tore at his skin, he was discovering the price of his folly.

The sounds of his pursuers grew nearer. Dunbar changed direction and plunged on through the jungle-like undergrowth. His breathing grew tighter and his limbs began to tire, but fear and the will to survive forced him on.

Then without warning he broke into a small clearing. He paused and listened. The hunt was falling behind. He gulped for air. Suddenly he became conscious of another, different sound—a low rasping hiss—like a pit full of rattle-snakes about to attack. In front of him the vegetation began to move. He backed away with a scream of fear. The Krynoid, now ten feet high and sprouting suckers and tentacles, detached itself from the surrounding bushes and advanced towards him. Panic-stricken, Dunbar pumped bullets into the towering mass of green, but they had no effect. It continued its relentless advance. Dunbar turned to run. As he did so he tripped in the dark over a hidden root and crashed to the ground. High above him the foul, hissing monster let out a blood-curdling screech and plunged downwards for the kill!

9

Siege

The Doctor and Sarah stopped in their tracks as several shots rang out. Then a ghastly scream filled the woods. The sound came from no more than a hundred yards away and the Doctor immediately set off towards it, tearing through the undergrowth at breakneck speed. Sarah stumbled after him.

Within a matter of seconds they were in the clearing. In the pale moonlight the Doctor made out a human body, barely recognisable, lying on the ground. Hovering above it, in full view, was the Krynoid.

The Doctor gripped his sword more tightly as the monster rose from its victim with a terrifying hiss and turned to face him.

'Doctor!' screamed Sarah as she rushed to his side. He quickly pushed her behind him for safety. Then the Krynoid let out a triumphant roar and started towards them.

It had advanced half way across the clearing when machine-gun fire suddenly broke out all around. The Doctor and Sarah threw themselves to the ground. The Krynoid faltered as bullets tore into its fleshy green exterior.

'Run to the cottage!' yelled the Doctor, and he and Sarah scrambled to their feet and dashed off.

Hearing the Doctor's command, Scorby ordered his men to follow, but one luckless guard was dragged off balance by a powerful snaking tentacle. With a scream he disappeared into the centre of the writhing, fibrous mass.

'Block the window!' ordered the Doctor as the others tumbled into the cottage. Two of the guards dragged a table across the room while the Doctor barricaded the door with heavy furniture.

'How do you do it, Doctor?' leered Scorby. 'You should be compost by now.'

'We'll all be compost if we don't keep away from that Krynoid.'

'Krynoid?' repeated Scorby in puzzlement. 'Is that what that thing is?'

Sarah turned to face him for the first time. 'Yes. And it used to be called Keeler,' she said bitterly. 'Remember your friend? Now do you see what we're up against?'

The colour drained from Scorby's cheeks. 'That's ... Keeler?' he stuttered in disbelief.

Sarah nodded.

At that moment Scorby's walkie-talkie started to bleep. 'Yeah?' he said, still sounding shaken.

'Scorby, what was all that firing?' The sharp, distorted voice of his master crackled through the room.

'It's the Krynoid, Mr Chase, it's got us trapped in the cottage.'

'You idiots! Listen to me—whatever happens it must not be harmed. Is that clear?'

Scorby gave the Doctor a hopeless glance. 'But you don't understand. It's ten feet high and it's already killed Dunbar.'

'I don't care who it kills,' screamed the voice hysterically, 'People are replaceable, the Krynoid is unique. It must not be damaged in any way. That is an order!'

The Doctor grabbed the walkie-talkie. 'Chase, try to understand one thing.' He spoke firmly and with authority. 'The Krynoid is an uncontrollable carnivore and it's getting bigger and more powerful by the minute ...' The receiver went dead. '... Chase! ... Chase! ...' The Doctor thrust it angrily back to Scorby. 'Arrogant fool!'

He strode to the window and peered out. He could see nothing, but the sinister alien rattle was clearly audible to everyone in the room.

'Just how big is this Krynoid thing going to get?' said Scorby, panic creeping into his voice.

'Oh, about the size of St Paul's cathedral,' replied the Doctor cheerfully. 'Then it will reproduce itself a thousandfold and eventually dominate your entire planet.'

Scorby's jaw dropped open and for once he was speechless.

The Doctor had moved away from the window during this exchange but now whirled round at the sound of splintering glass. The table blocking the window was hurled aside and a long green tentacle, about the diameter of a man's leg, snaked into the room. Pandemonium ensued as one of the guards started firing blindly. The tentacle thrashed from side to side knocking people and furniture in all directions. Then, catching hold of Sarah by the waist, it dragged her screaming towards the open window. Reacting quickly, the Doctor snatched up the sword and plunged it deep into the green proturberance. Its grip on Sarah slackened momentarily and the Doctor pulled her free. Then, as suddenly as it had entered, the tentacle withdrew.

'It can't get into the cottage,' explained the Doctor, gasping from his exertions, 'not for the moment at least. It's grown too big.'

He peered out again through the smashed window. The low, menacing rattle could still be heard. Everyone in the room was trembling from the shock of the attack, and looking to the Doctor for the next move. Cupping his hands round his mouth he leant out into the darkness and called, 'Stalemate for the present, Keeler. Can you hear me? Stalemate.'

There was a deathly hush and then the air was filled with a strange, hollow, rusty voice. 'The human ... was ... Keeler ... now of us ... now belongs ...'

The Doctor glanced at the anxious faces behind him in the room. 'I see. What do you want?'

'You, Doctor ... You are ... important ...'

'How kind. Thank you.'

'You have alien knowledge ... You must be the first ...'

Sarah took hold of the Doctor's arm. 'The first?'

'I think it means I've been singled out for special attention, Sarah.'

'Scorby!' called the booming voice, like a giant tannoy system surrounding the cottage, '... Give the Doctor to us ... your lives will then be spared.'

Scorby raised his machine gun. 'Sounds a fair deal to me, Doctor. How about it?' He took a threatening pace forward.

The Doctor stood his ground. 'If you kill me, Scorby, you're finished. Nobody else has any idea how to fight that creature.'

'I haven't heard any ideas from you so far,' snarled Scorby. His machine gun was still pointing at the Doctor's chest.

'Unless the Doctor gives himself up ... you will all perish ... You have two minutes ...'

All eyes in the room were trained on the Doctor. Sarah began to feel a prickly heat climb the back of her neck.

'Well?' Scorby slipped the safety catch.

'Fire!' said the Doctor abruptly. 'Fire is the only thing that might affect it.' He started to hunt among the debris, ignoring the gun still trained on his back.

'There's nothing here,' growled Scorby suspiciously.

'Oh yes, there is,' said the Doctor triumphantly, 'a spirit stove.' He blew the dust off it and unscrewed the top. 'You're going to make us a Molotov cocktail, Scorby, and lob it from the upstairs window when I give the word. This will distract the Krynoid long enough for me to slip out. Then with a bit of luck the

Krynoid will follow me and the rest of you will retreat to the safety of the main house. Quite simple, really.' He beamed a smile round the room.

Scorby looked unimpressed. 'It had better work, Doctor.' He began to empty the paraffin from the stove into an old milk bottle.

'Where are you going, Doctor?' whispered Sarah anxiously.

'Out—if I'm lucky. The worst part will be trying to convince some flat-headed Army type that the world is being threatened by an overgrown mangel-wurzel.' He turned away from the others in the room and lowered his voice. 'I'll have to risk leaving you behind, Sarah.'

Sarah nodded. It was more important now for the Doctor to organise a proper resistance to the Krynoid while there was still a chance of stopping it.

Scorby finished the makeshift incendiary bomb and climbed the stairs. The Doctor cleared the furniture from behind the main door and eased it open a fraction. The hoarse rattling of the Krynoid was drawing closer.

'Right, *now!*' yelled the Doctor and, yanking the door open, he hurtled out. Simultaneously there was a loud explosion and a sheet of flame lit up the interior of the cottage.

Running hard, the Doctor headed away from the cottage and into the dense black jungle. Behind him the Krynoid let out a bellow of pain and turned in pursuit. It was now at least twenty feet tall and, although possessing no limbs as such, its speed over the ground was astonishing. It slithered and glided through the trees like an advancing avalanche, smashing all before it.

As he plunged through the creepers the Doctor hoped his sense of direction had not deserted him. He was banking on finding the limousine which he and Sarah had abandoned many hours earlier.

Suddenly he was clear of the woods and standing on a gravel drive. With a gasp of relief he caught sight of the car still parked where he had left it. He bounded towards it and jumped into the driving seat. He could hear the trees crashing and toppling behind him and, above that, the angry roar of the Krynoid itself. Frantically he turned the key in the ignition. It wouldn't catch. Just as the roaring and hissing seemed almost on top of him the engine spluttered into life. Wrestling with the steering wheel, the Doctor spun the large car round and accelerated away.

As he did so, he caught the Krynoid in the full glare of the headlights. Its massive green trunk throbbed and pulsated, and the long clawing tentacles waved wildly in the air. In the split second it was discernible, this repulsive vision of unearthly terror burned itself into the Doctor's mind, never to be forgotten.

Then it was gone, and he was speeding through the cold black night in a race against time.

As the Doctor made his dash for freedom, Sarah and

the others slipped quickly from the cottage towards the safety of the main house. Once inside, Scorby posted guards and lookouts and led Sarah to the Laboratory. The room was deserted except for Hargreaves, looking slightly bewildered.

'Where's Mr Chase?'

'He went out. To try and get some photos, sir.'

Sarah registered surprise but Scorby, who was used to his master's bizarre ways, seemed unperturbed.

'All right, Hargreaves,' he nodded. 'Now listen ... get some timber from the workshop. We've got to barricade all these ground-floor windows. Understand?'

'If you say so, sir.' The butler departed on his errand.

Sarah glanced uneasily towards the window. 'He must have got away.' She tried to sound hopeful.

Scorby scowled darkly. 'He's no fool, your friend. He got out and we're still trapped.'

Stung by this remark, Sarah sprang to the Doctor's defence. 'He's only gone to get help. Somebody had to do it.'

'Sure,' came the sarcastic reply.

Sarah looked away. She felt very unsafe with this repressed psychopath. Better to keep quiet and avoid provocation. She sank into a chair and began the long wait for the Doctor's return.

Outside in the grounds Chase was moving cautiously through the undergrowth. He was still wearing an immaculate pinstripe suit, and round his neck hung an expensive-looking camera.

To the ordinary observer he might have appeared crankish, almost comical, but to those few who knew him his madness was not a ridiculous aberration but a deadly, all-consuming passion—a love of plant life above all other life forms, including human. Chase was physically repelled by people. He reduced contact with them to the bare minimum; hence the black gloves to avoid touching them, and the elaborate safety precautions surrounding the house to stop them getting in. Apart from his immediate entourage he was a recluse, known only by name to the outside world. But within the high walls of his own domain Chase had created a different world—a luxuriant, peaceful world of green—a world in which, for moments at least, he could pretend to shed his human guise and commune with his beloved plants.

It was such communion he now sought with the Krynoid, this strange and wonderful intruder from another planet. He, Chase, would divine its true intent and impart this knowledge to the rest of mankind.

He pressed on gently through the foliage. Suddenly there it stood, a towering fibrous mass of green, swaying slowly from side to side in the moonlight. As Chase approached, it seemed to sense his presence, and from beneath the wrinkled folds of its bark-like skin a glistening tendril snaked out towards him, menacingly.

'No! No! Not me,' cried Chase. 'I want to help. I want to help.'

The tendril wrapped itself around Chase and, lifting him bodily into the air, drew him in towards the cavernous folds of skin. Prodding suckers explored his body and face and he began to feel strangely drowsy. Then, just as he was on the point of suffocation, Chase found himself deposited once more on the wet grass. He lay there several minutes, gasping for breath. When he recovered the Krynoid had gone. He looked round, a weird unnatural glint in his eyes.

'Yes, yes,' he whispered. 'The plants must win. It will be a new world ... silent and beautiful.'

He rose to his feet and like a sleepwalker moved slowly away in the direction of the house.

10

The Plants Attack

It was just dawn when the Doctor brought the large limousine to a screeching halt outside the World Ecology Bureau. He leapt out and ran up the steps into the tall building. Behind, a posse of wailing police sirens indicated that his mad dash had not gone unnoticed.

Sir Colin was arguing with a spruce-looking Army Major when the Doctor burst in upon them like a whirlwind.

'Doctor!' gasped Sir Colin, completely taken aback.

'Where's the Brigadier?'

'Geneva,' answered the Major. 'I'm deputising. Major Beresford.' He bowed stiffly.

'What's going on down there, Doctor?' asked Sir Colin, gathering his wits.

'Revolution is going on. The Krynoid is growing larger and more powerful by the minute. What's more, if my guess is correct, all the rest of the vegetation on this planet will shortly turn hostile as well.'

A secretary entered and handed Sir Colin a piece of paper. As he read it he turned pale.

'This seems to confirm your theory, Doctor.' He read aloud. 'A gardener, an agricultural worker and a young woman have all been found strangled by plants within a mile of Chase's estate.' He looked up in dismay.

'The Krynoid is controlling them,' said the Doctor, his expression darkening.

The Major shook his head. 'I don't believe it.'

'I suggest you start believing it, Major,' snapped the Doctor. 'We're wasting time. I want you to organise flame-throwers, anti-tank guns and as many men as you can muster. Now!'

The Major jumped into action as if bitten by a dog.

'I'm going back straightaway—and I need some agricultural spray defoliant. I'll give you two minutes, Sir Colin. Get it down to the car.'

Sir Colin's office immediately became a hive of activity as the Doctor's orders were put into effect. Meanwhile, the Doctor picked up a phone and dialled a number he had memorised.

The phone rang loudly in the Laboratory, startling Sarah who had been sitting alone. Gingerly she picked up the receiver.

'Doctor!' Her face lit up. 'How did you . . . ?'

Interrupting her, he quickly explained what was happening. Sarah nodded, making mental notes as the Doctor issued instructions. Then suddenly they were cut off.

'Hello? Hello? Doctor?' Sarah jiggled the receiver up and down but the line seemed quite dead, as if the wires had been suddenly ripped out by someone.

Or something. Behind her a pane of glass cracked like a pistol shot. She spun round, dropping the phone in alarm. The window, which five minutes earlier had been clear, was now obscured by a mass of creepers. As she looked, the glass broke and the creepers inched their way into the room.

'What's happening?' cried Scorby from the doorway. He threw down a pile of timber.

'It must be the Krynoid. It's controlling the creepers!'

Another pane burst.

'Quick, help me board the windows,' shouted Scorby, and he began nailing the planks across.

As the two of them struggled to fight back the creepers, Hargreaves raced in. 'All the guards have gone!' he cried. 'I think they've made a run for it.'

'Just like a bunch of women,' growled Scorby.

'I also heard a scream from the West Gardens,' added Hargreaves. 'I didn't go out.'

Sarah looked concerned. 'We'd better investigate.' She started to leave.

'No. Stay put,' ordered Scorby. 'We can't risk it with that thing roaming about out there.'

Sarah scoffed. 'What was that you just said about women?' She ran from the room. Scorby hesitated, told Hargreaves to carry on boarding the windows, then followed Sarah out.

It was first light. Sarah's breath hung in the air as she made her way down the side of the house. Behind her she could hear Scorby's heavy footsteps on the grass. This time her own example had forced him to comply, but clearly when things got worse Scorby would be interested in saving only one skin—his own.

They were now nearing the thick undergrowth and had to pick their way carefully. Suddenly Sarah stopped. Sticking out of the long grass a few yards ahead was a human hand. Gingerly, she approached the body. A thick clump of trailing vines had wound itself tightly round one of the guards and strangled him to death.

'It's not possible,' whispered Sarah, looking round in horror. The vine creepers were swaying eerily from side to side although there was no breeze.

All at once a twig snapped underfoot. Startled, Scorby and Sarah whirled round. Chase was standing in the bushes a few feet away.

'I obtained some fascinating photographs,' he said. There was an odd, faraway look in his eyes.

Scorby ran to his side and shook his arm. 'Mr Chase, we're in desperate trouble. The plants are taking over!'

'Why not? It's their world. We animals are simply parasites after all.' Chase smiled strangely. 'I must get these developed.' He turned on his heel and hurried off towards the house.

Scorby shook his head. 'He's really gone.'

'He's been gone for years if you ask me,' replied Sarah quietly.

They retraced their steps to the Laboratory. Hargreaves had successfully blocked up the remaining windows. Chase's camera lay on the bench.

'Where is he?' said Scorby.

Hargreaves motioned towards the large ornate doors which led to the greenhouse. 'Talking to his plants. I wouldn't disturb him if I ...'

Scorby pushed the butler roughly to one side and threw open the doors. 'Chase!'

At the far end of the cat-walk, almost hidden by the dense foliage, was the immobile figure of his master. He was seated crosslegged, in the familiar Lotus position of an oriental mystic, eyes closed, hands pressed together beneath his chin. His lips were moving rapidly as if repeating a litany but no words could be heard because the room was filled with a piercing electronic sound.

Scorby crossed to the synthesiser and switched it off. Oblivious, Chase continued his incantation.

'We shall have perfection ... the world will be as it should have been from the beginning ... a paradise of green ...'

Scorby ran down the cat-walk and grabbed hold of the mumbling figure. 'Chase, listen to me!'

'... a harmony of root, stem, leaf and flower ...'

'*Chase!*'

'It's no good,' said Sarah. 'He's in some sort of trance.'

Scorby ignored her and continued to bellow at the inert form. 'Chase, you've got to understand. We're going to be trapped here unless we do something. Your precious plants are starting to kill people.'

Chase opened his eyes and gazed scornfully at the pleading figure before him. 'The time has come. Animals have held sway on this planet for millions of years. Now it is our turn.'

'What do you mean, your turn? You're one of us, Chase.'

'No he's not,' said Sarah. 'not any more.'

Scorby turned to Hargreaves. 'Come on. We've got to lock him up.' He started to grab Chase under the arms. The butler hesitated, his sense of loyalty uppermost.

Suddenly Sarah let out a shriek. 'Scorby! The plants! They're moving!'

As they looked the foliage on either side of the catwalk began to close in, cutting off their escape to the door. A creeper wrapped itself around Sarah's ankle. Desperately she jerked herself free. Another caught her arm. Scorby and Hargreaves also began to struggle. A sinister shrill rustling sound began to build up in the room, as if the plants themselves were emitting a battle-cry.

Someone began to choke. 'Help! Help!'

'Don't resist us. You have to die. All plant eaters must die.' Chase's hollow voice rang in Sarah's ears but now it seemed far, far away. The blood pounded in her temples, her muscles began to tire, she couldn't breathe, she was being slowly throttled to death!

11

Trapped!

'Sarah!'

Through a green haze she saw the blurred outline of the Doctor and felt a fine spray of liquid on her face. Around her the seething vegetation began to fall away. A second figure, dressed in khaki, swam into her vision, making for Scorby and the butler. The room was filled with a terrible keening wail, as if the plants were dying.

'Stop it! Stop it!' Chase's mad voice shrieked above the noise.

The Doctor reached Sarah and dragged her to her feet. Scorby too was free but the butler had disappeared beneath the writhing mass of leaves.

'Animal fiends! You'll pay for this!' Chase struggled desperately past them and ran from the room.

'Quick, get out,' ordered the Doctor, covering their exit with a jet of defoliant. The swirling mass of branches and creepers continued to harry them, but not so strongly, and they gained the safety of the Laboratory.

The Doctor banged the doors shut and hauled a heavy filing cabinet into position to secure them. The creepers were already poking through the gaps in the door.

'I feel like I've been pulled through a hedge backwards,' said Sarah, smiling weakly.

'What is that stuff?' asked Scorby, catching his breath for the first time.

'The latest military defoliant. Still on the secret list. Sergeant Henderson helped me scrounge a few cans from Sir Colin.'

'Nice to see you, Sergeant,' said Sarah, 'but are you all they could spare?'

'There's a unit on the way,' answered the Sergeant with a smile.

'Yes, and before they arrive we must clear the house of all plants,' barked the Doctor. 'They are the eyes and ears of the Krynoid.' He started to tear out the experimental trays containing plants and seedlings, and the others quickly followed suit.

Within minutes they had successfully disposed of a hundred or so plants into an outside courtyard.

'That's all we can find for the moment, Doctor,' said Sarah.

'Good. Back inside, everybody.'

As they turned to re-enter the house a loud roar reached their ears and the stone walls of the courtyard began to vibrate. For a moment it seemed the house itself was about to fall down.

Sarah looked up and there, towering above the roof-tops, was the Krynoid. It had grown to about sixty feet, and hundreds more tentacles protruded from its trunk-like body, each one capable of smashing a man to pulp.

'The door!' yelled the Doctor and he leapt to open

it. It wouldn't budge. Someone had locked it from the inside!

'Chase!' exclaimed the Doctor and hammered on the door. But it was solid Elizabethan oak. They were trapped.

'Look!' screamed Sarah.

The Krynoid had moved closer and one of its giant tentacles was poised to swoop down on them. This time there was no escape!

Suddenly, there was a blinding red flash and the Krynoid let out a screech of pain.

'It's the Major,' cried Sergeant Henderson. 'They're attacking it with the laser.'

They watched transfixed as bolts of red lightning slammed into the upper part of the monster. Distracted by this new threat the Krynoid turned from the courtyard and, letting out a deafening rattle, bore down on the small knot of soldiers operating the laser.

The Doctor saw the opportunity. 'Quick! Follow me.' He led the others at a gallop out of the courtyard and along the side of the house.

In the distance Beresford's commands rang out. 'Ready—fire! And another—fire!'

The Krynoid was advancing steadily despite the laser and, deciding discretion was the better part of valour, the Major ordered his men to retreat. As the khaki-clad figures scurried into the woodland the Krynoid gave a final roar of defiance and turned its attention once more towards the house.

The Major's diversion had created precious seconds

for the fleeing group to find another entrance, and they were now heading back to the comparative safety of the Laboratory.

'Well, at least the Major had a go,' said Sarah ruefully as they entered. 'Even if it was like using a peashooter on an elephant.'

Scorby, shaken by their narrow escape, sank into a corner. 'I never thought Chase was so far round the twist,' he muttered.

'Maybe he counted on the Krynoid sparing him if he sacrificed us,' said Sarah.

The Doctor shook his head. 'No. We were mistaken about who—or what—Chase is.'

The others stared at him.

'You said he went out in the grounds with a camera and came back unharmed. I should have realised. He locked that door behind us because he is acting as a plant. He's in league with the Krynoid.'

'Doctor, the radio's been smashed.' The Sergeant pointed to the broken apparatus which once kept Chase in contact with his patrolling guards.

'Now we're completely cut off,' whispered Sarah. Behind the doors leading to the greenhouse the trapped plants could be heard clawing and scratching on the polished metal.

'We've got to find Chase,' snapped the Doctor, 'before he does any more damage.' He strode out into the corridor. 'Sarah and I will take this wing ... you and Scorby check along there, Sergeant.'

The two couples set off in opposite directions along the dim passageway.

Sir Colin Thackeray, looking sleepless and tense in the early morning light, paced impatiently up and down the gravel drive by the gatehouse. The main house was invisible from where he stood and nothing had been heard of Major Beresford and his men after the initial burst of firing. Behind Sir Colin, anxious and expectant, a second unit stood ready for action.

Then, appearing at first in ones and twos, Beresford's troops began to emerge from the woods. Breathing hard the Major reported.

'We had to pull back. The laser was hopeless against it.'

'And you haven't made contact with the Doctor?'

'Not yet. He must be trapped inside the house. I'm going to try and sneak through with a couple of men.' He hurried off.

Sir Colin twirled his umbrella and pulled hard on the brim of his bowler hat. The Doctor was the only person with any idea of how to combat this alien menace. Somehow they had to get through to him.

Inside the house the Doctor and Sarah had covered the East Wing without coming across Chase. Now they linked up again with Scorby.

'No sign of him anywhere,' said Scorby. The Doctor

scrutinised his dark, sullen features. There was no telling whether he could be trusted—even in this desperate situation.

The Sergeant ran up. 'Doctor, there's a load of creeper breaking through into the corridor back there.'

'All right, we'd better retreat to the Lab.' The Doctor led them smartly away.

As they disappeared, the lurking figure of Chase stepped from behind a pillar and glided off into the gloom like an evil ghost.

Back in the Laboratory, the Doctor set about mending the two-way radio. Scorby crossed to the window and peered through a chink in the boards.

'It's like being under siege,' he murmured nervously.

'Yes,' the Doctor replied calmly. 'Soon the Krynoid will be large enough to crush the whole house. We haven't much time.'

As he spoke one of the wooden planks was forced away from the window, making Scorby jump.

'I'll try and find some more timber,' volunteered the Sergeant and hurried out.

'Be careful,' Sarah shouted after him.

The Sergeant made his way to the rear of the house where there was more likelihood of finding some spare wood. Too late he realised he was unarmed, he had left his rifle in the Lab. He decided to press on regardless.

Suddenly he thought he heard a noise. He stopped

and peered ahead. The passage was deserted. Then, without warning, a figure sprang from the shadows and struck him hard on the back of the head with a heavy metal spanner. Mercifully, that was the last the Sergeant knew.

Quickly his assailant dragged the unconscious body through a doorway, and moments later re-emerged, smiling malevolently. He closed the heavy door and vanished silently into the shadows. Within seconds a strange, muffled noise penetrated the door, like a heavy machine whirling into action, or a hungry monster devouring its prey.

'Any hope, Doctor?' Sarah peered anxiously at the tangle of wires.

'Chase didn't do any irreparable damage. I've nearly fixed it.'

'Well done, Doctor,' sneered Scorby. He was huddled on the floor like a man who had given up all hope. 'Why are you bothering? It's obvious your Army friends have scarpered. We're as dead as mutton.'

'Stop feeling sorry for yourself, Scorby,' said the Doctor, eyeing him distastefully.

Suddenly, the whole room gave a lurch, the radio shot out of the Doctor's hands and large pieces of masonry fell from the ceiling, smothering them all in a choking white dust.

'This looks like the final attack,' whispered the Doctor.

Scorby, sweating with fear, glanced towards the door.

'Don't be a fool, Scorby,' said the Doctor, guessing his intention. 'Everything that grows in the grounds is your enemy. You'll never make it.'

But Scorby's nerve had snapped. He scrambled to his feet and tore out before anyone could stop him.

Gripped with panic Scorby reached the East Wing and hunted for a door that would let him out. The Krynoid could not possibly be on this side of the house. All he had to do was make it to the wall.

He found a door and pushed it open. With a shock he ran headlong into a mass of creepers but somehow clawed a way through. Once out in the open he set off towards the heavy undergrowth which lay between himself and the main road. As he ran, he snatched a backwards glance at the house and gasped in horror. The whole West Wing, where the Doctor and Sarah were still trapped, was covered by the sprawling shape of the Krynoid, now over a hundred feet high. Its major limbs and tentacles had encompassed the roof and walls, like a giant spider sitting on its prey, and it was now beginning to slowly crush the solid masonry inwards. At the same time the surrounding vegetation had grown larger and wilder and was covering the house at the points the Krynoid could not reach, blocking every window and exit.

Scorby had just time to take all this in before he plunged headlong into the murderous jungle which still separated him from safety. Tendrils and branches flapped menacingly as he drove his way through. He was not far from the cottage and the stream that ran near by. Once across that he would be almost at the outer wall. Cursing and swearing he stumbled into the shallow water and struck out for the far bank. Fifteen ... ten ... five yards ... he was nearly there. Then, from nowhere, he felt a tangle of weeds wrap around his legs beneath the water. They were pulling him down! He lunged and thrashed about but the weeds were now around his body, trapping his arms, dragging him down, down, down beneath the icy water ...

With a final swirl the waters closed over Scorby's head and he disappeared below the surface. The writhing weeds subsided, their deadly purpose accomplished.

'Hello! Hello!'

The Doctor fiddled desperately with the radio tuner but all he got was an unfriendly crackle. He shook his head angrily, dislodging bits of plaster from his thick locks. 'Where's the Sergeant? I need the Major's wavelength.'

Sarah looked up uneasily. The Sergeant had been gone a suspiciously long time. 'I'll go and find him,' she said bravely. Before the Doctor could stop her she vanished down the corridor.

She had seen the Sergeant take the corridor towards the rear of the house, and she followed the same route.

Besides the continuous rattle of the Krynoid outside she could now hear another sound, a knocking from inside the large hot water conduits which ran all round the building and provided special heating for the plants. Here and there holes must have appeared in the pipes for small bursts of steam shot out periodically. She guessed the whole system must be overheating.

With a flicker of fear Sarah realised she was nearing the crusher room. There was something lying on the stone floor ahead. It was the Sergeant's green beret.

'Sergeant?

There was no response. The door to the crusher room stood open. Sarah crept up and peered in. The room was empty, the giant machine at rest. She stepped inside.

'Sergeant?'

A movement behind her made Sarah spin round. Leering at her, a heavy spanner raised high to strike, was the evil figure of Harrison Chase.

The Final Assault

'The Sergeant is no longer with us.'

'Chase!'

'He's in the garden. He's part *of* the garden.'

Sarah cast a glance of horror towards the crusher.

'We're both serving the plant world, the Sergeant and I—in different ways, of course. I have joined a life-form I have always admired for its beauty, colours, sensitivity. I have the Krynoid to thank for that, as it thanks me for its opportunity to exist and burgeon here on Earth. Soon the Krynoids will dominate everywhere ... your foul, animal species will disappear!'

'And you will all flower happily ever after.'

Chase's black-gloved hand gripped the spanner more tightly. 'You and your kind are merely parasites, dependant upon us for the air you breathe and the food you eat!' His voice grew hysterical. 'We have no need of you ...' He began to advance on her. Sarah cowered against the wall, raising her arms to ward off the blow she knew was coming. Then, in a state of pure frenzy, Chase leapt towards her.

The Doctor was inwardly cursing himself for letting Sarah go off alone as he twiddled with the tuner. Suddenly, the crackling gave way to a voice.

'This is Scorpio Section. I say again this is Scorpio Section. Are you receiving me? Over.'

It was the Major.

'Hello, Beresford. This is the Doctor. What action are you taking against the Krynoid? Over.'

'Hello, Doctor. The laser had no effect, but I managed to get nearer with a couple of men. The Krynoid is completely covering the house and beginning to crush it. All exits are blocked. I repeat, all exits are blocked.'

The Doctor gripped the microphone tightly. 'Listen, Beresford, by my reckoning you have less than fifteen minutes before the Krynoid reaches the point of primary germination.'

There was a pause at the other end. Then a new voice came on the line. 'Doctor ... Thackeray here. What do you mean, primary germination?'

'I mean the Krynoid is about to eject its spores— thousands of embryo pods like the ones we found in the ice. The whole Western hemisphere will be inundated with them.'

The Doctor heard Thackeray catch his breath. 'How can we stop it?'

'There's only one way now, Sir Colin. A low-level attack by aircraft with high explosives.'

'That will destroy the house too. What about you and the others?'

'Never mind us. Order that attack!' He switched off the receiver and headed for the door, his face a grim mask.

As he reached the doorway he paused and uttered a name softly beneath his breath, 'Sarah'. He had just signed a death warrant for the two of them.

Bound hand and foot, Sarah's inert form lay unconscious in the belly of the crushing machine.

'Three minutes. Go quietly, Miss Smith,' uttered Chase with a sadistic grin as he pulled the starter lever.

The giant machine shuddered into life. The gleaming steel rollers gathered speed and began to descend towards Sarah's defenceless body. As the crescendo of noise built up Sarah slowly stirred and opened her eyes. A spasm of inexpressible terror shot through her entire being. She was powerless to move or even scream. From the wall, Chase observed her without emotion.

Suddenly the door was flung open and the Doctor burst into the room. With a yell of fury Chase leapt at him with the spanner. Expertly the Doctor parried the blow and thrust Chase backwards into a pile of dustbins. Then, switching off the machine, he dived into it and lifted Sarah bodily to safety. As he did so Chase restarted the machine and hurled himself on the Doctor's back like a fiend possessed. The two men grappled precariously in the belly of the machine, inches away from the whirling blades.

'Switch it off, Sarah!' shouted the Doctor. Sarah tried to reach the lever but with her hands tied she could not stop it. The rollers spun faster and nearer. Finally, by sheer muscle power, the Doctor managed to lift himself clear and drop over the side to the floor. He tried to haul Chase after him, but the madman had caught hold of the Doctor's arm in a vice-like grip and was pulling him back. He seemed to possess the strength of ten men and the Doctor felt himself being drawn once again towards the grinding, chomping blades.

All at once, Chase let out a piercing yell and his iron grip slackened. His feet were trapped in the rollers and he was being sucked into the gaping maw of the crusher. Frantically the Doctor tried to pull him free but the monstrous machine would not disgorge its victim and suddenly, with a hideous scream, Chase was gone.

Shaking from his ordeal the Doctor staggered over to Sarah. 'I tried to save him,' he said. Sarah nodded mutely. Chase undoubtedly deserved to die, but it was not a death she would have wished on anyone. In a matter of seconds the Doctor had freed her and they left without a backwards glance.

High in the sky a tight formation of Phantom jets streaked across the South of England, heading for Chase's mansion. A curt, matter-of-fact voice crackled in Beresford's earphones.

'We'll be with you in three minutes, Scorpio Section. Over.'

'Roger Red Leader. Out.' Beresford clicked off his receiver and crossed to Sir Colin who was staring thoughtfully at the ground.

'The planes are on their way.'

'Is there nothing we can do to get them out?' Sir Colin's face wore a tortured expression.

Beresford shook his head sadly. 'Nothing. Nothing at all.'

'What are we going to do?'

Sarah was trying to keep up with the Doctor as he raced along the corridor. At every turn they were having to dodge falling masonry and crumbling walls as the Krynoid increased its stranglehold on the house. Its echoing roar grew louder.

'We're going to fight our way out, Sarah,' said the Doctor through clenched teeth, 'but we've only got about two minutes in which to do it.'

They were now at the rear of the building, where the Doctor had first entered, and he let out a grunt of satisfaction as they came upon the door. Gingerly he eased it open. A thick wall of vegetation completely blocked the exit and began to press forward into the corridor even as they stood there. The Doctor slammed the door shut and put his back against it. Sarah looked towards him in despair.

Suddenly the Doctor's eyes lit up. She followed his gaze. Several feet away was a door marked 'Boiler Room', and leading out of the wall in all directions were the large central-heating pipes Sarah had noticed earlier.

'Steam! Highly pressurised steam!' exclaimed the Doctor and he wrenched open the door. Inside was a bewildering collection of knobs and dials and, jutting out from the floor, the top of the boiler itself. Steam was spurting from it in little jets and the whole system seemed about to explode.

The Doctor grabbed one of the boiling hot pipes with his bare hands and prised it free of its connecting valve.

'Open the door when I tell you, Sarah ... and stand back!'

The Doctor gave another tug and the pipe tore away. Immediately a jet of superheated steam shot out of the end. '*Now!*'

As Sarah yanked open the door the Doctor carefully aimed the hissing, scalding jet at the thick tangle of creepers in the doorway. With a curious shrieking noise they began to wither and fall away.

'Follow me, Sarah!' yelled the Doctor and, flinging the pipe to one side, he plunged headlong into the foliage.

Overhead, the Phantoms screamed past on a low-level run. 'Hello, Scorpio Section. We see your target. We're coming in to attack now. Over.'

Beresford gave a last glance at Sir Colin who nodded imperceptibly. 'Understood. Out.'

The Phantoms banked and turned. 'OK. Here we go, chaps. Let's turn it into Chop Suey!'

They started their run in.

Head down and arms flailing, the Doctor hacked a path through the deadly jungle. The entire vegetation of Chase's estate seemed to have closed in on the house and every yard was an effort. The trees and plants seemed alive—snatching at their arms and tripping their legs—so that they bobbed about like corks in a sea of green. Exhausted and breathless, Sarah began to weaken and the Doctor had to haul her bodily through the murderous tangle. Overhead, the whine of the approaching jets rang in his ears. He redoubled his pace.

Just as the plants seemed about to overwhelm them they broke through into a clearing. Ahead, the Doctor spied a pile of sawn logs. With one last effort he dragged Sarah to safety behind them. Across the tops of the trees he could now see the Krynoid dwarfing the house, its massive tentacles reaching to the ground.

As he watched, the first of the jets streaked in overhead and loosed its rockets into the side of the building. There was a blinding flash and a huge explosion which devastated one entire wing of the house, but the Krynoid still remained, its tentacles waving furiously above the chimney tops.

A second Phantom screamed into the attack, then a third and a fourth. The Doctor and Sarah were hurled on their faces by the force of the explosions which rocked the ground and uprooted whole sections of woodland around them. Through the thunderous noise the Doctor suddenly heard the elephantine death-rattle of the Krynoid itself. The bombs must have hit it! A terrible, gigantic screeching filled the air then the noise ceased and everything went deathly quiet. The Doctor tapped Sarah's shoulder. Together they peered over the top of the logs. Chase's house, only a moment before enveloped by the mighty Krynoid, had vanished. The Krynoid too had disappeared and where they had both stood there was now only a smoking heap of ruins. The alien menace had finally been vanquished.

The Doctor and Sarah were seated comfortably in Sir Colin Thackeray's office, examining a battered roll of film.

'We found it in Chase's camera,' explained Sir Colin. 'The photographs are priceless now of course.'

'It's a wonder anything survived that inferno,' said Sarah, a note of sadness in her voice. The Doctor too looked rather glum, as if the strain of the last few hours had not yet passed from his mind.

'Well, Doctor,' said Sir Colin, trying to sound cheerful, 'do you think we've heard the last of the Krynoid?'

There was an awkward silence, then a faint smile appeared on the Time Lord's face. 'Hard to say, Sir Colin. You see, the Intergalactic Flora Society—of which I'm the honorary President—finds the Krynoid a difficult species to study. Their researchers tend to disappear.'

'I can imagine,' chipped in Sarah. 'A case of one veg and no meat.'

Sir Colin chuckled. 'Very neat, Miss Smith. By the way, speaking of societies, Doctor, the Royal Horticultural have got wind of this affair. They'd rather like you to address one of their meetings.'

'When's this?'

'They suggested the fifteenth.'

The Doctor took out his five hundred year diary and consulted it carefully. 'Sorry. Out of the question. The next couple of centuries are fully booked. Anytime after that.' He snapped the diary shut.

Sir Colin gaped at him. 'I never know when you're serious, Doctor ...'

'Send someone to talk to them about South American begonias. Much more the Royal Society's cup of nectar.' He rose hurriedly. 'Come along, Sarah.'

'Where are we going?'

'Cassiopeia.'

'Where?'

'A nice little spot for a holiday. It's time we had a break. Goodbye, Sir Colin.' Before she could argue further the Doctor gathered up his hat and scarf and strode out of the room.

Sarah turned to Sir Colin. 'Would you fancy a tiny excursion as well?' Her eyes twinkled with humour.

Sir Colin smiled back. 'I'd be delighted—but my

wife's expecting me home for tea.'

'Sarah!' the Doctor's voice bellowed from the corridor.

'I'd better go,' she whispered, 'he gets a bit tetchy now and then. It's his age, you know. Goodbye, Sir Colin.' Sarah gave a little wave and ran out of the room.

Sir Colin crossed to the window and looked out with a certain sense of relief. His attention was caught by an old-fashioned blue Police Box standing in the car park below. He was sure he had never seen it there before.

As he watched, the Doctor and Sarah emerged from the building and walked into the box. The light on top began to flash, a strange wheezing and groaning sound reached his ears and the Police Box vanished into thin air!

Sir Colin blinked, shook his head as if he had seen a ghost, and decided he was in need of a good, long sleep.

Contents

1

Vision of Death

*The telescopic-sight moved slowly across the crowded
hall. The glowing dot of light in the middle of the
view-finder paused, hovered, centred on an ornately-
robed figure in the middle of the central platform. A
finger tightened steadily on the trigger ... There was
the fierce crackle of a staser-bolt ... The President
jerked and crumpled to the floor ...*

'No,' shouted the Doctor. 'No!' He stood in the
centre of the TARDIS control-room, hands gripping
the edge of the control console. So vivid had been the
sudden hallucination that it took him a moment to
realise where he really was. The Doctor shook his
head dazedly, running long fingers through a tangle
of curly hair. 'First the summons to the Panopticon,'
he muttered. And now this ... What's *happening* to
me?'

It had all started at the end of yet another adventure
with Sarah Jane Smith, his young companion. They
were safely back in the TARDIS, about to return to
Earth, when the Doctor heard a deep, booming gong-
note echoing through his mind. It was a call no Time
Lord could ever ignore—the summons to the Panopticon. Returning the TARDIS to Earth, the Doctor
said a hurried farewell to Sarah, almost bundling her

from the control room. He realised she was more than a little hurt that their long friendship was being broken off so abruptly. But the Time Lord summons took precedence over everything else.

Once Sarah had been returned to Earth again the Doctor put the TARDIS on course for his home planet. Now, with Gallifrey very close, this sudden vision of assassination flashed into his mind ...

As he re-checked the instruments the Doctor's mind drifted back over the past. He remembered his youth on Gallifrey, the long years of training to fit him for the place on the High Council that seemed his unavoidable destiny. He remembered the steadily growing build-up of anger and frustration in his own mind at the never-ending ceremonials and elaborately costumed rituals, the endless accumulation of second-hand knowledge that would never be used. A final crisis had provoked rebellion. He had 'borrowed' the TARDIS and fled through Time and Space, determined to see the Universe for himself. After many adventures there had come capture, exile to Earth, and at last freedom again—his reward for dealing with the terrible Omega crisis. Now he was on his way back to Gallifrey, a planet to which he had once sworn never to return. Returning because, after all the long years of rebellion, at heart he was still a Time Lord!

The Doctor smiled wryly at the contradictions in his own nature—*and suddenly he was in the Panopticon again, forcing his way through the packed crowd, thrusting aside the robed figures that obstructed his path. A fleeting glimpse of astonished, shouting faces, and he broke away from the clutch of*

8

restraining hands ...

Now he was high up in one of the encircling galleries, the President's robed figure tiny on the platform below. Powerlessly he felt his own finger tightening on the trigger. There was the crackle of a staser-blast ... The President fell ...

... and so did the Doctor, rolling over as he hit the floor of the TARDIS. He struggled to his feet, and went to the console. The centre column had stopped moving. He was back on Gallifrey.

The approach of the TARDIS had been registered on one of the most advanced security scanning systems in the Galaxy. Now a metallic voice was echoing through the areas of tunnels and walk-ways known as the Cloisters, which connected the towers of the Capitol. 'Sector Seven alert. Unauthorised capsule entry imminent. Chancellery Guard stand to in Sector Seven.'

It reflects great credit on the Guard that they responded promptly and efficiently to this call. There were very few emergencies on Gallifrey, least of all within the Capitol, that impressive complex of Government buildings from which the Time Lord planet was administered. Usually the Guard's only function was to add colour and dignity to ceremonial occasions. Nevertheless, within minutes of the call they came pounding into the still empty Cloisters, spreading out in an armed cordon.

They waited tensely, keen alert young soldiers, hand-picked from the oldest families on Gallifrey.

Service in the Chancellery Guard was a keenly sought honour. A strange, wheezing, groaning sound shattered the silence, and a battered blue box appeared beneath one of the arches. Was this the dangerous intruder? Hands clutching their staser-guns in unaccustomed excitement, they waited for orders.

The Doctor studied the scanner, recognising his surroundings immediately. 'Right in the Capitol itself! They're not going to like *that*.' He adjusted the vision-field to take in the cordon of armed Guards. They looked dangerously keyed-up, capable of shooting him the moment he popped his head out. 'Now I'm in trouble. What a welcome! Surrounded by big-booted soldiers, the minute I get home.'

With impressive dignity, two officers made their way through the cordon, and marched up to the TARDIS. Senior in both age and rank was Castellan Spandrell, Commander of the Chancellery Guard, responsible for all security within the Capitol. He was a man of medium height, unusually broad and muscular for a Time Lord, with a heavy, impassive face that disguised a keen intelligence. Spandrell was a tough, sardonic character, made cynical by long years in Security. He had seen too much of the underside of Time Lord life to have any illusions about it, and his blunt no-nonsense manner had upset many a self-important Government official. Spandrell survived because of his integrity and his efficiency. No one else could cope with his difficult and thankless job. Beside Spandrell stood Commander Hildred, young, eager, and desperately keen to distinguish himself, overjoyed that the emergency had happened in *his* sector.

Hildred ran all round the TARDIS, like a terrier on the scent, and came back to Spandrell. 'You know, Castellan, if I didn't know better, I'd swear this was a Type Forty time capsule.'

Spandrell nodded. 'It is.' He looked at the TARDIS almost affectionately. He'd used a Type Forty himself in the old days. He thumped the side of the police box with a massive fist. 'Chameleon circuit appears to be stuck, though. Still, it's a wonder the thing's still in one piece.'

Hildred was staring wonderingly at the TARDIS. 'But it's impossible, Commander. There are no more Type Forties in service. They're out of commission—obsolete.'

The Doctor gave the TARDIS console a consoling pat. 'Obsolete? Twaddle. Take no notice, old thing!'

Spandrell's face filled the scanner-screen, and his voice boomed over the audio circuits. 'Nevertheless, Commander Hildred, this *is* a Type Forty TARDIS and it's landed in an unauthorised zone just before a very important ceremony. I want the occupants arrested.'

The Doctor sighed.

Spandrell stepped back to take a better look at the TARDIS. 'Now, as I remember, the barrier on this model is a single-curtain trimonic. You'll need a cypher-indent key to get in.'

Hildred came to attention, clicking his heels. 'Very

good, Castellan. I'll send for one at once.'

Spandrell looked thoughtfully at him. He was reluctant to leave matters to Hildred, who was both over-eager and inexperienced, but at this particular time there were many other duties claiming his attention. Still, if he left full instructions ... 'After you've arrested the occupants, put them in safe custody, and impound the machine.' Surely that covered everything, thought Spandrell. Even Hildred couldn't go wrong with such a simple task.

Hildred saluted. 'Very good, Castellan. Will you want to question the prisoners?'

'Eventually, Hildred, eventually. But *not* on Presidential Resignation day.' Spandrell moved away.

Inside the TARDIS, the Castellan's last words were echoing in the Doctor's mind. 'Presidential Resignation Day ...' *The hovering rifle-shot settled on its target. The President crumpled and fell* ... Hallucination—or premonition? The Doctor looked at the scanner screen, and the encircling Guards. If he came out now he'd be thrown into a cell and forgotten until the Ceremony was over. Somehow he had to get past those Guards, and warn the President ...

Castellan Spandrell made his way to the Archive Tower, home of the Capitol's Records Section. The Tower was actually one enormous computer, and as he entered the readout room, Spandrell was impressed, as always, by the air of timeless calm that filled this part of the Capitol complex. All around him data banks quietly hummed and throbbed, while soft-footed Recorders moved unhurriedly to and fro. As Spandrell entered, Co-ordinator Engin bustled forward to greet him. Engin was old, even for a Time Lord, not only in the number of his regenerations but in the physical age of his present body. He had spent all of his lives in the Records Section, beginning as a humble data Recorder, rising slowly through the centuries to his present eminence. Engin's present body was almost worn-out now, and he was bent and shrunken with age, his hair snowy-white, his face wrinkled like an old apple. His next and probably final regeneration was long overdue. But Engin constantly refused to take the time away from his duties, insisting that since he never left the computer area anyway, his present body would serve for a year or two yet.

Despite his great age, Engin was still brisk and efficient, and his eyes were alive with curiosity. 'This is a great honour, Castellan. How may I be of service to you?'

Spandrell replied with equal formality. 'Just a little information, Co-ordinator. If I could have a terminal?'

Engin ushered him to a secluded booth, made a quite unnecessary check on the terminal controls, then busied himself with the study of a data bank—not quite out of earshot.

Spandrell touched a control in front of him. 'Data retrieval. Request information on all Type Forty time travel capsules currently operational.'

There was a moment's silence, then the calm,

emotional computer voice said, 'Negative information. Type Forty capsules are all de-registered and non-operational.'

Spandrell considered. Computers, even Time Lord computers, didn't really think. They could usually tell you what you asked, but they never volunteered information, never saw through to the reasons behind your question. A computer was a kind of idiot genius. You had to make all your questions very clear, because the computer would tell you exactly what you asked —and nothing more.

Carefully he formulated his next request. 'Report number of de-registrations.'

'Three hundred and four.'

'Report original number of registrations.'

'Three hundred and five.'

Impatiently Spandrell snapped, 'Report reason for numerical imbalance.' Under his breath he added, 'You stupid great tin box.'

'One capsule removed from register. Reference Malfeasance Tribunal order three zero nine zero six. Subject—The Doctor.' Spandrell sat brooding for a moment, his heavy features set and grim. Unable to restrain his curiosity any longer, Engin wandered casually across to him. 'Can I be of any further help, Castellan Spandrell?'

'One moment, Co-ordinator.' Spandrell tapped out a code on his wrist-communicator. Seconds later the face of Hildred appeared on the tiny screen. 'Commander Hildred, Sector Seven.'

'Malfeasance, Hildred.'

'Castellan?'

14

'*Crime*. The occupant of your Type Forty is a convicted criminal known as "The Doctor". Approach with extreme caution.'

Hildred lowered his own viewer and turned to the waiting Guards at his side. 'You heard that? Set your stasers. Safety off.' The Guards adjusted the settings on their staser-guns. From now on, they would be shooting to kill. Hildred spoke into his communicator. 'I want armed reinforcements in Sector Seven. Immediately, please.'

The Doctor was writing a brief note on a sheet of parchment embossed with an elaborate seal. He finished, signed with a flourish, and glanced in the scanner. A Guard was approaching Hildred, carrying a flat leather case. As Hildred opened the lid, the Doctor glimpsed row upon row of keys set into the black velvet lining. He smiled ruefully. On any other planet in the Universe the TARDIS was invulnerable. But not on Gallifrey—the planet on which it had been made.

He flung open a nearby locker, and started rummaging through it in search of inspiration. Somewhere near the bottom, he found a dusty cardboard box, with Turkish lettering on the lid. 'Cash and Carry, Constantinople,' translated the Doctor. An idea was forming in his mind. 'After all,' he thought, 'it worked for old Sherlock . . .'

The Doctor touched a control, and the lights slowly

dimmed. From the cardboard box he took a hookah, an elaborate Turkish water-pipe with a long flexible stem. He carried it over to the high-backed armchair that stood near the console.

After several unsuccessful attempts, Hildred found exactly the right key, and turned it in the TARDIS lock. The door swung open. Staser-pistol in hand, Hildred moved cautiously into the TARDIS control room, armed Guards behind him.

Peering through the gloom, Hildred saw a high-backed chair on the far side of the control room. Its back was angled towards him, but he could just make out a relaxed figure lounging in the chair. It had a broad-brimmed hat tipped over its eyes, an immensely long scarf dangled from its neck and it seemed to be puffing at a complicated, long-stemmed pipe. The air above the chair was blue with smoke.

Hildred stepped forward, staser-pistol raised. 'Don't move!' The figure didn't move, and as Hildred came closer he saw why. The shape in the chair was no more than a pile of cushions, the hat was propped up against the chair-back, and the long flexible pipe-stem was held by a knot in the scarf. Deceived by the simplest of illusions, Hildred had seen what he expected to see.

(The Doctor crouched motionless in the shadows behind the console. As Hildred and his Guards crowded round the chair, he rose silently and edged his way towards the door.)

There was a square of white pinned to one of the

cushions—a note. Hildred snatched it up. He was about to read it when he saw a flicker of movement on the TARDIS scanner. A tall figure was disappearing into the darkness of the Cloisters. 'There he goes!' shouted Hildred. 'After him!' Guards at his heels, Hildred dashed from the TARDIS.

The Doctor sprinted along the Cloisters trying desperately to recall boyhood memories of forbidden games, of hide-and-seek. Now, if he could get into the main tower by one of the service lifts ... He turned a corner, and there was the lift-door, right in front of him. He touched the call button and there was a faint hum of power. A moment later the lift doors slid open—to reveal a Guard, staser-gun at the ready. The first of Hildred's reinforcements had arrived.

The Guard raised his rifle. The Doctor stepped back, thinking this must be the shortest and most unsuccessful escape of his career.

A staser-gun crackled, and the Guard staggered sideways and toppled out of the lift. The Doctor turned, caught a fleeting glimpse of a cowled figure disappearing into the darkness. 'Stop!' he called ... but the figure was gone. As the Doctor turned to look at the body of the Guard, he heard shouts and the clatter of booted feet.

Hildred and his Guards were almost upon him—and he was standing over the dead body of one of their fellows ...

2

The Secret Enemy

The Doctor hesitated for no more than a moment. The death of the Guard made flight more urgent than ever. No one would believe in his innocence. He'd be lucky if he wasn't shot down on the spot.

Leaning forward, the Doctor stretched out a long arm, and pressed one of the control buttons inside the lift ...

Hildred and his men ran up just in time to see the lift doors close. After a brief examination of the Guard's body, Hildred straightened up, his face grim. 'He's got into the main tower. We'll have to search every floor.'

He raised his communicator. 'All Guards report to Main Tower, Sector Seven. Armed and dangerous intruder at large! You are authorised to shoot on sight!'

The Doctor, however, wasn't in the lift. He'd sent it speeding, empty, to the top floor of the tower. Now, hiding in the shadows around the corner, he slipped quietly away.

Co-ordinator Engin sat hunched over a read-out terminal studying the flickering of symbols across the screen. Spandrell looked on impatiently. Information in this category was automatically encoded, but Engin had worked so long with the computer that he could sight-read the symbols. Spandrell was in a hurry and he found it infuriating that all his information had to be filtered through the sometimes wandering mind of the ancient Co-ordinator.

Engin screwed up his eyes as he peered at the symbols. 'Now, let me see ... It appears that in view of certain extenuating circumstances, the Tribunal chose to impose a lenient sentence.'

'*What?*' asked Spandrell impatiently.

Literal as one of his own computers, Engin began again. 'In view of certain extenuating circumstances ...'

'No, no, Co-ordinator. I meant what *sentence?*'

Engin chuckled wheezily. 'I do beg your pardon. It appears the sentence was one of ... exile to Earth!'

'Earth?' Spandrell had never heard of the place.

'Sol 3—in Mutters Spiral. Interesting little planet, I understand. Been visited by several of our graduates ...'

'Is there any further information—anything *relevant?*'

A fresh line of symbols appeared on the screen. 'There is a rather interesting addendum, Castellan. It seems the sentence was subsequently remitted. The Doctor was given a complete pardon—at the intercession of the Celestial Intervention Agency.'

Spandrell looked up sharply. This gave the whole affair a new and worrying dimension. The whole basis of Time Lord philosophy was that there must be no interference in the affairs of the Universe. Yet from time to time such interference was thought urgently necessary. These operations were under the control of an ultra-secret Agency, composed of Time Lords of the highest rank, and they were always shrouded in mystery. 'Does it say why the Agency interceded?'

'I'm afraid not. All it says here is, "Refer to Omega file"—and that's restricted. High Council only.'

Spandrell had been on a remote province of Gallifrey at the time, but the effects of the terrible Omega crisis had been felt even there. The attack from some unknown all-powerful enemy, the crippling energy-drain that had almost destroyed the planet—then suddenly it was all over, and everyone was pretending it had never happened. Only the President and a few members of the High Council knew the full story. If the intruder had been mixed up in an affair of such magnitude, he was no ordinary criminal.*

Perhaps the Doctor's early life would provide some clue, thought Spandrell. 'Can you get me his biographical extract?'

'Certainly. It'll take a moment or two to withdraw it from the files.'

Engin went to a panel in the wall nearby, and began adjusting controls. As Spandrell waited impatiently, he saw Hildred moving hesitantly towards him. He could tell by the expression of the young Commander's face that the news wasn't good.

Hildred was a conscientious young officer and he felt it his duty to report his failure in person. He came to a halt before Spandrell and saluted. 'Castellan, I

* See 'Doctor Who—The Three Doctors'.

have to report that in the matter of the intruder in Sector Seven ...'

'Well? Where *is* he?'

Hildred gulped. 'He evaded us, Castellan. He shot one of my Guards.'

Spandrell closed his eyes briefly, as if in pain. 'I see. Such efficiency.'

'We have him trapped in the main Communications Tower, Castellan ...'

'Well done, Hildred!' said Spandrell bitingly. 'You receive adequate early warning that an antiquated capsule is about to arrive in your section—in the very heart of the Capitol. You are then informed that the occupant is a known criminal ... whereupon you allow him to escape and conceal himself in a building a mere fifty-three stories high. A clever stratagem, Hildred. I take it you're trying to confuse him?'

Hildred winced under the blast of sarcasm. 'My apologies, Castellan. The responsibility is mine. He won't escape capture again.'

Spandrell sighed. 'Let us hope not. In view of your record so far, you'd better not make rash promises.'

Hildred was holding out a square of parchment. 'I found this inside the capsule, Castellan.'

Spandrell took the note and read it aloud. '"To the Castellan of the Chancellery Guard: I have good reason to believe that the life of His Excellency the President is in danger. Do not ignore this warning— The Doctor."' He held the note up to the light. 'I see he's signed it over the Prydonian seal.'

There was a whoosh of compressed air and a muted chime. Engin opened a circular metal hatch in the

21

wall and took out a silvery tube with a red cap. 'Indeed? Well, he has every right to do so. It appears that your intruder is—or was—a member of that noble Chapter.'

'How can you tell?'

Engin tapped the red cap. 'All biographies are colour coded according to Chapter.'

Spandrell took the cylinder and stared at it thoughtfully. 'Are they now? I had no idea ...'

Engin gave a wheezy chuckle. 'No? I suppose your duties usually involve you with more plebeian classes, eh, Castellan?'

Spandrell smiled ruefully. There was more than a little truth in the old Co-ordinator's jibe. The Time Lords were themselves a kind of aristocracy. Relatively few inhabitants of Gallifrey were of Time Lord rank. And this élite group was itself sub-divided into a number of societies or Chapters, Prydonians, Arcalians, Patrexes, and so forth. The members of each Chapter were bound together by a complex web of family and political alliances, and by one over-riding purpose—to compete with all the rival Chapters. And of all the different Chapters, the Prydonians were the most aristocratic, the most powerful, and the most ruthless.

The Castellan tapped the little silver tube against his palm. 'A Prydonian renegade, eh? We're in deep waters, Hildred. I think I'd better refer this to Chancellor Goth.'

The Doctor found it relatively easy to elude the departing Guards. Convinced he was already inside the Tower, they made no attempt to look for him in the Cloisters. He made his way quietly back to the TARDIS and slipped inside. As the door closed behind him, a black-cowled figure watched from the shadows. Its voice was a dry, rasping croak. 'As ingenious as ever, Doctor—and as predictable.' The cowled figure glided away, swallowed up by darkness.

Spandrell always felt clumsy and out of place in the Chancellor's office, surrounded by marble columns, silken hangings and fine mosaics. Behind an immense, ornately-carved desk, Chancellor Goth listened to Spandrell's account of the mysterious intruder.

Goth was tall, handsome, immensely impressive in his elaborate robes. There was no sign on his impassive face that he was worried, or even particularly interested by the story.

'This Doctor seems to be a Prydonian renegade,' Spandrell concluded. 'When a Prydonian forswears his birthright, there can be little else he fears to lose —isn't that so, sir?'

Goth nodded slowly. He was a Prydonian himself, and knew the truth of Spandrell's remark. 'So you think the danger is real?'

'He's already killed one of my Guards. I think he's ruthless and determined, sir. And if he's involved with the Agency ...'

'That's just it, Castellan. If he *is* in their service, why should he wish to harm the President?'

Spandrell shrugged. 'He could have been suborned by some outside force. If he's been false to his Prydonian vows his fidelity is already suspect.'

'But the note,' persisted Goth. 'Why warn us in advance?'

'To put us off balance—get us looking the wrong way for some reason. Prydonians are notoriously——' He broke off.

Goth gave one of his rare smiles. 'Devious, Castellan? Not so. We merely see a little further ahead than most. Now then, what is it that you want from me?'

'Your permission to withdraw fifty Guards from the Panopticon—to help search the Communications Tower.'

'It will mean a certain loss of pomp and ceremony...'

Spandrell sighed. An assassin on the loose, and the Chancellor was worrying about appearances. 'I'm afraid so, Chancellor. But I'll feel happier once this intruder is in custody.'

'Very well, Castellan. If you must ...'

Spandrell bowed. 'Thank you, sir.' He began a hasty withdrawal, before the Chancellor could change his mind.

Goth detained him, a hand on his arm, 'I'd rather like to see this—TARDIS, you called it? Extraordinary to think an old Type Forty could still be operational.'

'It's in the Cloisters, sir. Sector Seven.'

To Spandrell's surprise, the Chancellor accompanied him towards the door. 'Then we'll have to hurry. I have an audience with the Cardinals in a few minutes.' Cardinals were the senior officials of the various rival Chapters. They played a vital part in the complex organisation of the Resignation Day Ceremonies. Spandrell bowed resignedly, and followed the Chancellor from the room.

The Doctor fiddled irritably with the tuner of his scanner. 'I've got to know more about what's going on ... Now, where's that local news circuit ... ah!'

The interior of the Panopticon Hall appeared on the little screen. This immense, circular chamber, used by the Time Lords for all major ceremonies, occupied the entire central dome of the Panopticon. Row upon row of viewing galleries ran round the walls. The marble floor was big enough to hold an army, the domed glass roof so high overhead that one lost all sensation of being indoors. On the far side of the hall, an enormous staircase led from the robing rooms down onto the central dais. Here the President would finally appear, to announce his resignation, and name his successor.

The Doctor saw that the camera was set up on one of the upper service galleries. From this height the figures on the floor of the Panopticon looked like animated chessmen, as the officials of the various Chapters, gorgeous in their multi-coloured robes, filed into position on the floor of the Chamber.

A solemn voice was commentating on the proceedings. 'Around me on the floor, and in the high galleries of the Panopticon, the Time Lords are already gathering in their ceremonial robes with the traditional colourful collars. The orange and scarlet of the Prydonians, the green of the Arcalians, the heliotrope of the Patrexes, and many others ... The one question that is on all their lips, the question of the day as his Supremacy leaves public life—who will he name as his successor?'

The camera zoomed in on a small plump figure standing by the main door of the Panopticon. The Doctor groaned. 'I might have known. It's Runcible! Runcible the fatuous ...'

Long, long ago, Runcible and the Doctor had been at school together. Even in those days Runcible had been utterly fascinated by rituals and traditions. No wonder he'd finished up in Public Record Video, the one position that would allow him to attend as many ceremonies as he liked.

With pompous reverence, Runcible continued his commentary. 'Approaching now is Cardinal Borusa, Leader of the Prydonian Chapter—the Chapter that has produced more Time Lord Presidents than all other Chapters together—and perhaps he will give us his answer to the vital question.'

A tall, hawk-faced old man, in the robes of a High Cardinal, was sweeping across the floor, flanked by a group of lesser officials. His face was seamed and wrinkled, and his hair snowy white, but his bearing was still upright and his eyes sparkled with intelligence. This was Cardinal Borusa, one of the most eminent figures in Time Lord public life. He had twice been offered the office of President, and had twice refused. The Presidential post had too many purely ceremonial functions. Borusa preferred to exercise real authority from behind the scenes.

The Doctor saw Runcible step forward. 'Cardinal Borusa, if you could spare a moment, sir——'

Borusa stopped and looked down at Runcible in mild astonishment. 'Yes?'

'Public Register Video, sir. If I could have a few words?'

Borusa peered keenly at him. 'Good gracious! Runcible, is it not?'

Runcible smiled, flattered at the recognition. 'That's right, sir.'

Borusa turned to the others. 'Runcible was one of my old pupils at the Prydonian Academy.'

'May I offer my congratulations on your recent elevation to High Cardinal, sir?'

'Thank you, Runcible. Good day to you.' Borusa moved on. As far as he was concerned, the interview was over.

Runcible scurried after him. 'Wait, sir—if I could just ask you a few questions——'

Irritated by this second interruption, the formidable old man snapped, 'Runcible, you had ample opportunity to ask me questions during your singularly mis-spent years at the Academy. You failed to avail yourself of the opportunity then, and it is too late now. Good day!'

Borusa strode off, followed by his entourage. For a moment Runcible was totally deflated, reduced to a delinquent schoolboy. Then he took a deep breath and smiled winningly into the unseen camera. 'I'm afraid Cardinal Borusa cannot, at this present point in time, commit himself to a reply. However, according to my own sources, Chancellor Goth, senior member of the Prydonian Chapter, and present number two in the High Council, is the widely fancied candidate.' Runcible paused and looked round. 'Approaching now are the Cardinals of the Patrexes Chapter ...'

Runcible droned on, but the Doctor wasn't listening. His eyes were fixed on the grand staircase. Down that staircase soon would come the President ...

The assassin pressed the trigger. The President crumpled and fell ...

Angrily the Doctor shook his head, and the vision faded. The ceremony hadn't started yet, the assassination hadn't happened. Somehow the Doctor had to get out of the TARDIS and stop his terrible vision from becoming reality.

3

Death of a Time Lord

In the Panopticon, Runcible was still droning on. 'Oh, shut up,' said the Doctor irritably and switched back to scan the Cloisters outside the TARDIS. All was still and silent, mist drifting eerily between the arches.

Three figures appeared out of the gathering darkness. Castellan Spandrell and Chancellor Goth walked side by side, Hildred following respectfully behind them.

As they approached, Goth was saying, 'I take it there is no way the intruder can enter the Panopticon from the Tower?'

Spandrell shook his head. 'Not without the help of an accomplice.'

As they came to a halt before the TARDIS, Goth said, 'You're suggesting there may also be a traitor within?'

'Perhaps the Doctor has gone inside the Tower to shake off the Guards, while someone else lifts the barriers that will admit him to the Panopticon.'

'What an inventive, suspicious mind you have, Spandrell. Though I suppose it's natural, in your position ...' Goth studied the TARDIS.

'So this is a Type Forty? Fascinating!'

'The shape is intended to be infinitely variable,

Chancellor. This one seems to have got stuck.'

'Yet it's still operational. Remarkable! What are you going to do with it?'

'I hadn't really thought. I've been more concerned with the occupant.'

'Well, I shouldn't leave it standing here—he might try to sneak back inside. Have it transducted to the Panopticon Museum. Most appropriate place, eh?' With a nod, Goth strode away.

Spandrell turned to Hildred. 'Get a transducer operator here right away.' Hildred used his wrist-communicator, and a few minutes later an overalled technician appeared, carrying a heavy box. From it he produced four black discs, magnetic terminals, which he attached to the TARDIS. He raised his communicator. 'Transduce to Capitol Museum—now.'

Somewhere inside the Communications Tower, another technician operated controls, the transducer beam locked on, and the TARDIS vanished slowly in sections—top left-hand corner, top right-hand corner, bottom left-hand corner—the final section, and it was gone.

Inside the Panopticon Museum, the TARDIS reappeared, section by section, just as it had vanished. The door opened and the Doctor staggered out, hands to his head. 'What a way to travel,' he thought indignantly. Satisfied that, like the TARDIS, he'd arrived in one piece, the Doctor looked round. He was in a big gloomy room, filled with glass cases, holding all kinds of strange objects. The place was obviously a storeroom for items not currently on display. The Doctor rubbed his chin. At least he was inside the Panopticon. The next step was to get to the main hall without being captured. The Doctor looked at the strange collection of objects all round him. There were old carvings, bits of regalia, even an old grandfather clock. Just beside it was a dusty glass display case. It held a kind of rudimentary dummy, wearing elaborate golden ceremonial robes. The Doctor smiled . . .

Deep beneath the Archive Tower two allies were conferring in a hidden chamber. One stood by the doorway, wrapped in a black cloak, the other sat, robed and cowled, in a high-backed stone chair. The room was in darkness, and any observer would have seen only two dark shapes, talking in low voices.

'So,' hissed the huddled shape in the chair. 'He is within the Capitol?'

'All his actions are exactly as you predicted, Master.'

'I know him,' croaked the cowled figure. 'I know him of old.'

'And are you sure he will succeed in reaching the Panopticon?'

'Of course. The Doctor is very resourceful. He knows he is entering a trap—but how can he resist such a bait.'

'The hope of preventing an assassination?'

'Exactly. Quixotic fool. He will die quickly.'

The Master leaned forwards, and the watcher by the door shrank back at the sight of the crawling horror of his ravaged features. The cracked, wizened skin, stretched tight over the skull, one eye almost closed, the other wide open and glaring madly. It was like the face of death itself, he thought.

'Remember,' insisted the Master, 'afterwards he must die *quickly*. See to it!'

The figure by the door bowed, and moved away.

Spandrell waited impatiently by the Cloister lift, as the door opened and Hildred emerged. 'Well?'

'We checked the entire tower, Castellan. All fifty-three floors. Nothing.'

Spandrell snorted. 'It's hardly surprising. I've been doing some checking myself. Take a look at this. Guard!'

At Spandrell's shout a Guard hurried forward, carrying a wide-barrelled, torch-like device. This was a track-tracer, a device which could follow the recent passage of living beings over inanimate material. It produced a high-pitched wailing sound which varied in volume with the strength of the track.

At a nod from Spandrell, the Guard demonstrated the Doctor's movements—up to the lift, and then away, over to the dark corner.

'He never even went into the lift,' whispered Hildred. 'He just doubled back.'

'That's right,' said Spandrell wearily. 'Back to the capsule. It's the only place for him to go. You'd better come with me, Hildred.' He turned to the Guard. 'You too. We'll need your tracker.'

Spandrell raised his communicator. 'Transduction section? I want to know *exactly* where you sent that capsule. Yes, the Type Forty from the Cloisters.'

Hildred and the Guard behind him, Spandrell led the way into the museum and up to the TARDIS. He nodded to the Guard, who began scanning with the tracker. The wailing sound led them away from the TARDIS and over to a glass case.

It was labelled 'Gold Usher,' and a placard inside explained the important part which this official took in many ceremonies. But instead of high-collared golden robes, the dummy in the case was wearing a loose roomy jacket. A long scarf dangled from its neck, and a floppy broad-rimmed hat perched on its round, featureless head.

Spandrell said grimly, 'Now we know how he plans to get into the Panopticon Hall.'

'But the Guards—everyone has to show a pass.'

'Do you think they'll stop Gold Usher?' snarled Spandrell. 'Would you, Hildred? Get over there and find him.'

'Right away, Castellan!' Beckoning to the Guard, Hildred set off at a run.

'And Hildred,' called Spandrell, 'try to be discreet!'

Hildred had already gone. Spandrell sighed and plunged his hands into the pockets of his tunic. He felt an unfamiliar shape and drew it out. It was a red-capped silver tube—the Doctor's biographical capsule. Perhaps somewhere in the intruder's past there was a clue to his present purpose. Trying to forget his aching feet, Spandrell set off for the Achives section.

In a velvet-curtained robing area, close to the main

hall of the Panopticon, two very old Time Lords were changing into ceremonial robes, and holding a vague conversation. 'You know,' said one, proudly, '*I* can remember the inauguration of Pandak the Third.' As he spoke, he was struggling out of his everyday robes. The ceremonial robes of a Prydonian Cardinal hung on a special stand nearby—that is, until a long gold-clad arm appeared from behind the curtains and lifted them quietly off.

The second Time Lord nodded vaguely, 'Pandak the Third, eh? Well, well . . .'

'Nine hundred years *he* lasted, you know. Now there was a President with some staying power.' The old Time Lord looked round at the empty stand. 'Where's my gown? I could have sworn it was here a moment ago.' He looked in total bafflement at the now empty stand. He became aware of a figure slipping through the curtains, and standing behind him. 'Here you are, sir.'

Grateful for the unexpected help, the old Time Lord slipped his arms into the offered robe, settling it onto his shoulders. His mind was still on the past. 'Thank you, my dear fellow, most awfully kind.' He settled the robe on his shoulders, as the tall figure slipped away. 'Nine hundred years,' he repeated. 'Bit different from these fellows today, chopping and changing every couple of centuries.' He noticed his fellow Time Lord staring at him. 'Anything the matter?'

'Well—you're *not* Gold Usher, are you?'

The Time Lord sighed. Clearly his old friend was getting a bit past it. 'Of course I'm not! I'm a Pry-

34

donian Cardinal, you know that.' He looked down at his robe and was astonished to find it gold, instead of the familiar orange and scarlet. 'I say,' he spluttered indignantly, 'that fellow's given me the wrong gown.'

'What fellow?'

The old Time Lord pulled back the heavy drapes. But the Doctor had gone.

The automatic Public Record Video camera was still functioning, perched on its ledge in the upper service gallery. But there was no sign of the technician who should have been looking after it.

On the wide shelf formed by the balcony edge, two black-gloved hands were expertly assembling a light staser-rifle. Stock, barrel, energy-cylinder and telescopic sight were all clipped efficiently into place.

When the rifle was complete, the black-cowled figure rested its elbows on the balcony edge beside the camera. Through the telescopic sights it began scanning the ever-growing crowd on the floor down below it. It amused the Master to think that with a gentle pressure on the trigger he could bring death to any one he chose.

Spandrell tapped the silver tube and looked at the old Co-ordinator. 'There must be *something* in his history, *some* clue. If I can convince Chancellor Goth that the threat is serious ...'

'My dear Castellan, it would have to be very serious before they'd delay the Ceremony at this late date.

By now the President must be well on his way to the Panopticon. Still if you'll pass me the data-coil ...'

Spandrell took the red cap off the tube and shook out the double-spiral of fine silver wire upon which all the known details of the Doctor's lives were micro-encoded. He was about to pass it over when he paused, peering closely at it. 'This has been in a reader—very recently!'

'Surely not. If your intruder has just arrived ...'

Spandrell held up the coil. 'Look! No trace of mica dust.'

'There are millions upon millions of extracts in the data-files, Castellan. It's hardly feasible that some-one would chose to extract this particular one *before* the intruder arrived—and since then, it has been in your hands.'

'I live with the dirt of the past, Co-ordinator. And I can tell you, the dust of old crimes besmirches the fingers.'

Engin shook his head in puzzlement. 'Well if it has been withdrawn there'll certainly be a record. I can run a trace if you like.'

'I'd certainly like to know who had it. But the extract itself is more urgent. Let's see that first.'

'A pleasure, Castellan.' Engin slipped the silver coil into a reader, and the Doctor's lives began to flow across the screen.

The wandering telescopic sight froze on a tall figure in Prydonian robes, entering the Panopticon Hall by a side door.

There was a dry, rasping chuckle. 'There he is at last. The innocent to the slaughter!'

The Doctor looked round the crowded hall, and was appalled to see Hildred and a squad of Guards coming through the main door. With any luck they would still be looking for Gold Usher. But the Doctor felt conspicuous on his own, and he looked quickly round for someone to talk to.

A small plump figure stood rather disconsolately by the wall. Runcible had finished his preliminary transmission, and now had nothing to do until the ceremony proper began. The Doctor marched up to him and flung a friendly arm around his shoulders. 'Runcible my dear fellow! How nice to see you again.' With a gentle but remorseless pressure he swung Runcible round so they were facing away from the approaching Guards.

Runcible looked up at the Doctor in some annoyance. 'I'm sorry, I don't believe I recall ...'

The Doctor looked hurt. 'I know it's a long time since we were at the Academy together. And of course, I've changed a good deal. But surely you remember me? They used to call me the Doctor ...'

Runcible frowned. 'I still don't believe ... I say, weren't you expelled or something? No, not expelled, I remember you at graduation. But you were involved in some scandal, later on ...'

Cursing Runcible's too-accurate memory the Doctor said hurriedly, 'Oh that's all forgiven and forgotten now, old chap. Back in the fold!'

'Really?' said Runcible sceptically. 'And where have you been all these years?'

'Oh, here and there. Round and about, you know.'
As the Doctor spoke he was gazing over Runcible's
shoulder, following the progress of Hildred and his
Guards as they forced their way through the ever-
growing crowd.

Runcible sensed his distraction. 'Is something the
matter?'

'No, nothing, nothing. I get the odd twinge occa-
sionally.'

'Well, if you will lead such a rackety life,' said
Runcible disapprovingly. 'I suppose you've already
had several regenerations?'

'Yes, quite a few, I'm afraid ...'

Runcible felt he'd spent enough time on this odd
and probably rather shady figure from the distant past.
'Well,' he said insincerely, 'nice to have talked to
you. Must get on. I'm doing the Public Record Video-
cast, you know. We resume transmission soon.'

The Doctor saw that Hildred had paused and was
looking all around him. He laid a detaining hand
on Runcible's arm. 'I know—and I think you're doing
an absolutely *splendid* job.'

'Do you really think so?' Runcible couldn't help
feeling pleased. All too many Time Lords treated the
Public Record Video as a pointless nuisance.

'I do indeed,' said the Doctor earnestly. 'You've got
a natural gift, you know. Somehow you have a marvellous way of making the whole thing come alive.'

There was a sudden fanfare, and Runcible
panicked. 'The President's arrived outside the Panopticon. He'll be coming down the main stair at any

moment.' He raised his wrist-communicator and jabbed at the controls.

The Doctor was staring into space. *The President jerked back and crumpled to the ground* ...

At this precise moment, the President was standing in the lift, surrounded by his retinue. The lift was carrying him to a corridor by the head of the great stairway, purely and simply so that he could make an impressive entrance, sweeping down the stairs and onto the central dais. An usher was handing him a smooth black rod, and settling the wide metallic links of the traditional Sash of Rassilon around his shoulders.

'You have everything you need, sir?' he asked discreetly. 'The list?'

'What? Oh, the Resignation Honours list.' The President touched a scroll inside his robes. 'Yes, here it is. One or two names in there will surprise them!'

The lift came smoothly to a halt, the doors opened and the President emerged into the antechamber at the head of the stairs. The usher nodded to a waiting aide. 'The President is ready. Let the ceremony begin!'

Runcible jabbed savagely at his communicator controls. 'Come on, *answer*, you stupid oick!'

The Doctor seemed to come to. 'What is it, Runcible? Having trouble?'

'No, my camera technician just isn't answering. I should be getting a signal from him—up there.'

Runcible pointed, and the Doctor looked up. High above the Panopticon Hall, on the topmost service gallery, he could see the squat shape of a video camera. The Doctor's eyes narrowed. And there was something else. *Projecting beside the camera was the barrel of a staser-rifle.*

'No!' shouted the Doctor. He set off across the floor of the Panopticon at a run, knocking Time Lords aside like skittles. Hands reached out to stop him, but he broke free of their hold. Dimly he remembered that this too had been part of his vision. 'They'll kill him!' Forcing his way through the crowd the Doctor made for the staircase that led to the service galleries.

Hildred's attention was attracted by the disturbance. He turned, just in time to see the Doctor disappearing. 'There he goes,' yelled Hildred. 'After him!' Followed by his Guards, Hildred too began forcing his way across the crowded hall.

The buzz of outraged comment from the assembled Time Lords was brought to a halt by another fanfare. Runcible remembered his duty. Hoping desperately that the video camera was still working, he began speaking softly into his communicator.

'There seems to have been some kind of disturbance here in the Panopticon Hall—no doubt we shall hear the full story later. Now the ceremony is about to begin. The members of the High Council, led by Chancellor Goth, are already assembled on the dais to greet his Supremacy the President ...'

Heart pounding, legs aching, the Doctor ran up and

up and up, ascending the service stairs at astonishing speed. He reached the top at last, and sprinted along the upper service gallery towards the video camera. Gasping for breath, he reached it at last ... and stopped in astonishment. The video camera hummed quietly on the edge of the balcony, the staser-rifle resting beside it. But there was no one in sight. Perhaps he'd already frightened the assassin away ...

The Doctor went forward and looked over the balcony. Below him was the main dais, and there was the President, making his stately way through the ranks of the High Council. The Doctor had an excellent view, though the balcony was so high above the dais that he could see little more of the President and High Council than the tops of their heads.

The members of the High Council were crowding round the President to greet him ... The Doctor could hear pounding feet as Hildred and his Guards ran along the gallery. The Doctor smiled, making no attempt to get away. He was still in a certain amount of trouble. But somehow he'd talk his way out of it. After all, what could they charge him with? Parking the TARDIS in a restricted zone? The main thing, he'd arrived in time. The President was safe.

Suddenly the Doctor tensed. Staring intently below him, he snatched up the staser-rifle, threw it to his shoulder, and fired. A staser-blast echoed through the Panopticon. The President jerked, staggered backwards. His lifeless body crumpled to the floor.

4

Trapped

The Doctor stood staring numbly down onto the floor of the Panopticon. It was a scene of utter chaos. Time Lords milled about in horrified panic, and on the dais, the members of the High Council crowded round the fallen President, hiding the body from view.

When Hildred's Guards burst into the service gallery, the Doctor was still standing there, the rifle in his hands. The leading Guard raised his staser-gun to fire. 'No!' shouted Hildred. 'Take him alive!'

The Doctor turned to run but now it was too late. The Guards hurled themselves upon him and there was a confused struggle. The butt of a staser-pistol took the Doctor behind the ear, and he fell at Hildred's feet.

On the dais, Goth was cradling the President's body in his arms. Runcible forced his way to the edge of the group. 'Did you see what happened, sir?'

The Chancellor shook his head dazedly. 'Not really. There was a shot, and the President fell. I was right beside him.'

Runcible turned to Cardinal Borusa. 'Is the President dead, sir?'

Even Borusa seemed stunned. 'I fear so. We live in terrible times.'

Runcible saw Spandrell shouldering his way through the crowd. 'Castellan Spandrell, can you tell us what's happening?

Spandrell ignored him. 'Will you all keep back please? Make way!' Behind Spandrell came Hildred and his Guards, two of them half-dragging, half-carrying the semi-conscious figure of the Doctor. 'Is that him, Castellan?' asked Runcible excitedly. 'Is that the man?'

The Doctor was dragged up to the little group of High Councillors. Borusa looked at him incredulously. 'Is this the assassin? A Prydonian?'

Hildred said triumphantly, 'There's no possible doubt, sir. We found him in the camera-gallery. He was holding this.' He showed them the staser-rifle. There was an angry murmur from the crowd, and they began crowding around the Doctor. Spandrell turned to Hildred. 'Get him out of here, you fool. Put him in the detention sector.'

Suddenly the Doctor opened his eyes and gazed muzzily at Spandrell. 'Is the roof still there? I could have sworn it fell in on me!'

'Take him away,' ordered Hildred.

As the Guards dragged him out, the Doctor started to struggle. 'Wait! I can help you. I saw the whole thing ...' Still struggling and protesting, the Doctor was hauled away.

By now horrified Panopticon attendants were removing the President's body. Goth rose from beside the stretcher and beckoned to Spandrell. The

Chancellor's handsome face was cold and bleak. 'Castellan, the President is dead. The trial of the assassin will be held immediately.'

'I need more time, Chancellor.'

'Time for what?'

'There are unanswered questions. About the assassin, about his motives.'

'Such questions will be answered at the trial.'

Cardinal Borusa came across to join them. 'I agree with the Castellan, Chancellor. Too much haste is against all our traditions of justice.'

'This is no ordinary crime. This is a constitutional crisis. The President died before he could name his successor. In these circumstances, we are legally bound to hold an election within forty-eight hours.'

Borusa's legalistic mind refused to accept Goth's reasoning. 'The trial of the assassin, and the choice of the new President, are two separate issues,' he began ponderously.

Fiercely Goth interrupted him. 'Not so, Cardinal. This is a political matter. At the moment, the Time Lords are leaderless and in disarray. The assassin must be tried and executed *before* the election—to prove to Gallifrey that the High Council are still in control.'

Stripped of his borrowed Prydonian robes, the Doctor was in his shirt-sleeves, clamped to the walls of a metal cell, a fierce blue light playing into his eyes. The light came from a small torch-like device in the hands of Commander Hildred, and it seemed to burn into the

Doctor's brain. Sweat broke out on his face, and he twisted in pain. 'You will confess,' said Hildred remorselessly.

'All right,' gasped the Doctor. 'I confess!'

The light was shut off. 'Very sensible, Doctor.'

The Doctor smiled with dry lips. 'I confess you're a bigger idiot than I thought you were.'

Immediately the blue light was boring into his brain again. 'There are fifteen intensity settings on this device, Doctor,' snarled Hildred. 'At the moment you are only experiencing level nine. You would do better to talk.'

'I've ... nothing ... to say,' gasped the Doctor.

The light-beam stabbed at him again, more fiercely this time. Through a haze of pain he heard Hildred's voice. 'I'm sure you'll think of something soon.'

Spandrell came into the cell, and looked enquiringly at Hildred, who said eagerly, 'Just give me a little more time with him, Castellan.'

Spandrell said, 'Turn that thing off—and get out.' Hildred stamped out of the cell, slamming the door behind him. Spandrell looked after him with disgust. It was bad enough that they were sometimes forced to use such methods. To enjoy the process was unforgivable.

He crossed to the Doctor's slumped figure and lifted an eyelid. 'Are you all right?' Slowly the Doctor's eye focused and he said weakly, 'Tweedledee?'

Spandrell wondered if the interrogation had affected the Doctor's brain. 'I'm sorry?' He released the wall clamps and the Doctor sank weakly onto a metal bench. 'I must apologise for my subordinate,' said

45

Spandrell calmly. 'He lets his enthusiasm run away with him.'

'Tweedledum and Tweedledee,' muttered the Doctor. 'The hot and cold technique. You're not very original.'

'We're simply seekers after truth, Doctor. And we don't have very much time. Chancellor Goth has ordered your immediate trial.'

The Doctor rubbed his aching head. Despite the rough handling, he could feel his strength coming back. His mind was starting to work again. He looked at Spandrell. 'I'd like to help you, if I can. I suppose you'd like a signed confession?'

'That would be a help. I have a tidy mind, Doctor. Even when a conviction is certain, I hate to go into court without knowing all the facts. Motive, for instance.'

'Now there's a sensible question. Why should anyone want to murder a *retiring* President?'

'Some personal grudge?'

The Doctor smiled. 'I never met him.'

'I know Doctor. I scanned your biographical data.'

'And yet you still think I did it?'

'I think you're going to be executed for it,' said Spandrell calmly. 'They're preparing the vaporisation chamber at this very moment. You have about three more hours to live.'

The Doctor sat up. 'That's monstrous. Vaporisation without representation is against the constitution.'

'Well, frankly Doctor, you're a political embarrassment.'

The Doctor found that the prospect of execution

46

concentrated his mind wonderfully. 'You realise I've been framed, Castellan?'

'Framed?'

'Yes, *framed*. It's an Earth expression. It means someone has gone to a lot of trouble to get me into this mess.'

'All right, Doctor. Just how did someone "frame" you into being up in that gallery with a freshly fired staser-rifle in your hands?'

The Doctor told of the sequence of events that had led him to the gallery. 'I looked down on to the dais— *and saw one of the High Council take a staser-pistol from under his robes and aim at the President.* Don't ask me which one—I couldn't see their faces. *I shot at the assassin.* I missed—and he didn't.'

Spandrell looked thoughtfully at the Doctor. There was something strangely convincing about this renegade. 'Tell me, why *did* you come back to Gallifrey— if it wasn't to assassinate the President?'

'To save his life. If you remember I left a note— which, presumably you did nothing about?'

'I did all I could. So, you knew the President was going to be assassinated?'

'In a way, yes. I—experienced it.'

'Go on.'

The Doctor sighed. 'This is the bit you're not going to believe ...'

Co-ordinator Engin stared fascinatedly into the little screen of Spandrell's video-communicator. It was switched to playback, and on the tiny screen the Doctor was saying, 'This is the bit you're not going to believe. People talk of a premonition of tragedy, but I saw it happening. I saw the President die, as vividly, as clearly as I see this room now.'

Then Spandrell's own voice. 'And where were you when this happened?'

'In the TARDIS, travelling in Vortex. It was just after I'd heard the summons to the Panopticon.'

Spandrell switched off the communicator. 'Well, what do you think?'

The old Time Lord shook his head. 'True precognitive vision is impossible.'

'He knows that, and he knows we know it. Yet he maintains it happened—— And whatever he is, the Doctor isn't a fool.'

'So you believe this story of his?'

Almost reluctantly Spandrell said, 'I'm beginning to.'

'Nobody else will!'

'I think he's been framed.'

'Framed?'

'It's an Earth expression, Co-ordinator. You were going to run a check for me—on who'd withdrawn the Doctor's data coil recently.'

'Nobody had. I'm afraid you were wrong there Castellan.'

'I very much doubt it,' said Spandrell obstinately.

'The machine is virtually infallible. Data extraction is impossible without an operating key. The code of the particular key is recorded against the archive number of the data extract. My key is the only one recorded against the Doctor's number—when I withdrew the data at your request.'

'How many of these operating keys are there?'

'They are issued only to the High Council. No one else is allowed access to Time Lord data extracts ... except of course for yourself, Castellan, in the line of duty.'

'Suppose the record has been erased?'

Engin was shocked. 'Clearly, you have no idea of the complexity of exitonic circuitry.'

'No, I haven't. But suppose somebody else has—— Is it *possible*?'

'Theoretically yes. But it would require an unprincipled mathematical genius with an unparallelled knowledge of applied exitonics.'

Spandrell smiled wryly. 'Well, that narrows the field, Co-ordinator. There can't be many of those on the High Council.'

In the council hall of the Chancellery, the Cardinals were assembling for the Doctor's trial. Chancellor Goth sat at the head of the long table, Cardinal Borusa at his side. While the other Cardinals were taking their places, Goth and Borusa argued in low voices. 'I still feel we should allow time for reflection, Chancellor, time for passions to cool,' said Borusa stubbornly.

Goth's voice was unyielding. 'A wise and beloved President has been shot down in his last hours of office. No amount of reflection is going to alter that.'

'Nevertheless, in the present emotional climate,

49

there is danger that a violent action will cause an equally violent reaction.'

'I am aware of your concern for justice, Cardinal,' said Goth patiently. 'And of course I share it. But there are other considerations.' He paused, choosing his words. 'There is some possibility that, after the election, I shall have the honour of being President of the Council.'

'You're being over-modest, Chancellor,' said Borusa drily. 'Everyone knows the President would have named you as his successor. Everyone will feel that in electing you they are simply carrying out his wishes.'

Goth waved the compliment aside. 'Who can be sure what was in the President's mind? But that apart, it is our inviolable custom for an incoming President to pardon all political prisoners. Is the new President to pardon the murderer of his predecessor—or break with an age-old custom? Either course would be difficult. We can only avoid the dilemma by seeing that this sordid affair is concluded before the new President takes office.'

Borusa was unimpressed. '*All* Presidents must face difficult decisions, Chancellor. It is by their decisions that they are judged.'

Goth's face darkened, and he seemed about to make an angry reply. But at this moment the Doctor was brought in, and the Court Usher sounded the call for the trial to begin.

As the Doctor listened to the proceedings, he reflected that his trial wasn't likely to be a long one. With crisp efficiency, Spandrell told of the early warning that had alerted them to the Doctor's unauthorised arrival. Hildred told of his entry into the TARDIS, and of the unsuccessful search that had followed. He told of the hunt through the hall of the Panopticon, of discovering the Doctor in the service gallery, staser-rifle in hand, seconds after the President's death.

With the main story established, there followed various corroborating witnesses. Runcible told of meeting the Doctor in the Panopticon. 'I thought he seemed nervous, apprehensive. He was looking round all the time we were talking. Just before the President appeared, he started to run across the floor ...'

An old and indignant Time Lord told of the Doctor's mad dash to the staircase. 'He pushed past me in a loutish and unmannerly way. I caught his arm to remonstrate with him but he pulled away shouting, "Let me go. They'll kill him."'

Goth leaned forward. 'Forgive me sir, but are you perhaps getting a little hard of hearing?'

'At my age one must expect these things. I'm nearing the end of my twelfth regeneration, you know. As a matter of fact, I've been having trouble with my hip recently—and my back ...'

Goth cut across the list of symptoms. 'So the prisoner *might* have been saying, "Let me go, I'll kill him"?'

'Well, it's possible ... he *might* have said that ...'

For the first and only time in the trial the Doctor exercised his right to question witnesses. 'I believe you said I shouted, sir?'

'That's right.'

'And you can hear a *loud* voice clearly enough?'

'Yes, of course I can.'

'Thank you, sir,' said the Doctor and sat down again. For the remainder of the testimony he sat quietly, doodling on the pad in front of him.

When all the evidence had been given, Chancellor Goth conferred for a moment with his fellow members of the High Council. Then he looked sternly at the Doctor. 'Have you anything to say before our verdict is reached?'

Spandrell watched the Doctor get up. He wondered how the High Council would react, when the Doctor made his astonishing charge that the real assassin was one of their number. However, like everyone else in the Court, Spandrell was quite unprepared for what happened next.

The Doctor paused, looked round the room then spoke in a loud clear voice, 'I have only one thing to say. I wish to offer myself as a candidate for the Presidency of the High Council.'

5

The Horror in the Gallery

There was a moment of shocked silence—then pandemonium. Goth's angry voice cut through the babble.
'*What* was that?'

'I offer myself as a candidate for the Presidency,'
repeated the Doctor. 'And I invoke Article Seventeen
of the Constitution ... the guarantee of liberty. No
candidate for office shall be in any way barred or
restrained from presenting his claim.'

'The guarantee of liberty does not extend to the
protection of assassins—you have no right to claim it.'

Borusa leaned forward, with an expression of
malicious enjoyment. 'Forgive me, Chancellor, but as
an expert in jurisprudence, I must disagree. The
accused has not yet been found guilty. Until he is, the
protection of Article Seventeen still applies.'

'He is using his cunning to abuse a legal tech-
nicality.'

The Doctor said cheerfully, 'Nonsense. I'm claiming a legal right.'

Borusa agreed. 'This trial must now stand adjourned
until after the election.'

There were many more angry protests from Chancellor Goth, but Borusa was immovable. The law was
the law. Finally Goth rose to his feet. 'Very well. It

appears that the prisoner must be set free until the election is over.' He looked menacingly at the Doctor. 'Do not think you will escape justice. Immediately after the election, you will be re-arrested, tried and executed. Castellan!'

Spandrell rose from his corner and came forward. Like Borusa he was sardonically amused by the turn of events—though, unlike Borusa, he didn't dare to show it. His face impassive, he said, 'Yes, Chancellor?'

'See the accused has no opportunity to leave the Capitol.'

Goth stormed out of the Courtroom, and the other Cardinals began filing after him. Spandrell went over to the Doctor, who was quietly doodling on his pad. 'Well, Doctor, you have forty-eight hours!'

The Doctor smiled wryly. 'It's a lot better than three, isn't it?'

'What are you going to do with the time?'

'Prove my innocence. Find the real assassin. If I can convince you I didn't do it—will you help me?'

Spandrell looked down at him. 'You know, I can't help admiring your audacity. Very well, Doctor— convince me!'

The Councillor descended the stone steps to the secret chamber where the cowled figure sat immobile in the high-backed chair. It might not have moved at all since the last time they met. 'Well?' croaked the rasping voice.

'The trial was adjourned, Master. He pleaded Article Seventeen, the clause of protection.'

He heard the sound of the Master's painful breathing ... 'He remains as ingenious as ever.'

'He will not escape for long.'

'Escape is not in his mind,' whispered the Master. 'Now he is hunting *you*!'

There was panic in the Time Lord's voice. 'It was a mistake to bring him here. We could have used anyone ...'

'No. We could *not* have used anyone. You do not understand hatred, as I understand it. Only hate keeps me alive. Why else should I endure *this*?' The Master stretched out a hand that might have belonged to a mummified corpse, withered skin stretched tight across the bones. 'I *must* see the Doctor die in shame and dishonour, before I destroy the Time Lords. Nothing else matters. *Nothing* ...' The agonised whisper of hate drifted through the shadows of the underground room.

The Castellan and his staff occupied a set of old-fashioned chambers in an obscure corner of the Capitol, as plain and functional as Spandrell himself. The Doctor stood before a battered wooden table. On it rested the staser-rifle he had been holding when he was captured.

The Doctor picked up the rifle and Spandrell stepped back cautiously. 'I hope you're not planning anything ambitious, Doctor.' He nodded towards the door where Hildred stood with a knot of Guards.

'Wouldn't dream of it, old chap. I just wanted to

be sure it was the same rifle. Are you a good shot, Castellan?'

'It's part of my job.'

The Doctor nodded thoughtfully. 'Yes ... I'm a pretty good shot myself as it happens.' He pointed towards an old-fashioned light-globe set into the far wall of the long room. 'You see that light?'

'What about it?'

'Try to hit it.' He tossed the rifle to Spandrell, who caught it automatically. 'Go on—just try!'

Spandrell gave him a baffled look then raised the staser-rifle to his shoulder. 'People get run in for this sort of vandalism,' he muttered.

He peered through the telescopic sight and centered the glowing white dot on the light-globe. At this range the shot was ludicrously easy. Spandrell squeezed the trigger. The bark of the staser-blast *should* have been followed by the sound of shattering crystal. But it wasn't. He saw to his astonishment that the light-globe was still there on the wall. He moved closer. The scorch-mark of the staser-blast wasn't even on the wall. It was on the ceiling just above.

'The sights have been fixed,' said the Doctor simply. 'I couldn't have hit the President with that rifle if I tried. More important, I didn't hit the real assassin when I did fire. That's *why* the sights were fixed.'

There was now only one question in Spandrell's mind. '*Which* member of the High Council shot the President?'

'I told you—I was almost directly above. Those high collars hid their faces.'

'Why didn't you tell your story in court?'

56

'With the real assassin as one of my judges?'

Spandrell nodded, sinking wearily into a chair. 'So we're after one of the High Council? It's a good story, Doctor. But it's still only a story. Where's your evidence? The rifle isn't enough by itself.'

The Doctor was striding about the room. In his mind he was seeing the scene in the service gallery. The staser-rifle resting on the ledge, the deserted video camera humming quietly away ... 'I'll tell you where the evidence is,' he shouted. 'In the Public Register camera. I was standing right beside it. Blow up the image and we'll be able to identify the assassin ...'

Spandrell jumped up. 'Doctor, you may end up as President yet. Hildred, come over here. I want you to escort the Doctor to the Panopticon.'

'Now sir? It's late, it'll be closed up.'

'I'm aware of that. I'm going to get the Chancellor's authority to open it. I'll want Commentator Runcible as well. Get everyone over there and wait for me.'

Despite the late hour, Goth was still hard at work when Spandrell arrived at the Chancellery. He received the Castellan at once, and listened in astonishment to his request. 'You want the Panopticon opened —at this hour? That's rather unusual. For what reason?'

'Further investigation, sir,' said Spandrell woodenly. He had no intention of repeating the Doctor's wild story until there was solid evidence.

'I see. Well of course, Castellan, if you think there is any more to be discovered ... I'll give the necessary orders.'

'Thank you, sir.'

57

'You're keeping a close watch on this Doctor?'

'Someone with him all the time, sir.'

Goth was shuffling papers in evident irritation. 'You realise, Castellan that the Doctor and myself are the *only* candidates in this election?'

'Is that so, sir?'

'*I* am to compete with a renegade and a murderer! It exposes the highest office in the land to ridicule. My first action as President will be to order Cardinal Borusa to amend Article Seventeen. I'll see this sort of thing never happens again ...'

When Spandrell arrived at the Panopticon the Doctor, Runcible and Hildred were all waiting for him. A scandalised Panopticon attendant appeared to open the doors. Since the huge building was now in semi-darkness, Spandrell bullied the attendant into producing a supply of hand-lanterns. Armed with these they entered the cavernous darkness of the enormous hall, their footsteps echoing on the marble floor. They made their way on to the dais and stood grouped around the spot where the President had fallen. There was something curiously pathetic about the sprawled outline that marked the place of his death.

Runcible was protesting about being dragged out in the middle of the night. Spandrell told him why he was wanted.

'Well, it's not really my field,' said Runcible dubiously. 'My technician would normally handle that sort of thing.'

'Your technician has disappeared, Runcible,' said

Spandrell patiently. 'I take it you do have *some* technical knowledge? All I want to see is the sequence leading up to the actual assassination.'

'Yes ... well, I expect that will be stored in the last band of the drum.'

'Splendid,' said Spandrell sardonically. 'Then perhaps you will be kind enough to go and fetch it?'

'Er ... yes. Right, Castellan. Now?'

'If you please, Commentator Runcible.'

Runcible's light bobbed away as he set off for the stairs.

High above in the service gallery, a dark figure watched his approach.

The Doctor was studying the chalk outline. 'So, if the President was standing about here ... and the assassin about here ... and I fired from up there ... the bolt would have passed over his head, and to the left ...'

'Then let's look for the blaster mark,' said Spandrell practically. He shone his lantern. 'Somewhere across here, I should say ...'

'Castellan!' called Hildred.

'What is it?'

'I thought I heard movement up in the service gallery.'

'That's only natural, Commander. After all I've just sent Runcible up there. Now come and help search for this blaster-mark.'

Hildred obeyed, but he was still puzzled. If it *had* been Runcible—why hadn't he seen his lantern?

Runcible was glad when he finally reached the upper gallery. It had been an eerie journey, alone through the darkness. All the way along the service gallery he'd been thinking he heard—*sounds*.

He looked over the balcony and saw the lights of the others bobbing about down below. With a sigh, Runcible turned to the video camera. As far as he could see, no one had interfered with it. Clumsily he began unscrewing the drum that housed the recorder-bands.

It was Hildred who found the blaster mark. 'Here Castellan!' He shone his lantern at the point where the rear wall of the dais joined the floor.

They came across to join him, and the Doctor peered at the modest-sized scorch-mark. 'Is that it?'

'Stasers don't do a lot of damage—except to body tissue,' said Spandrell. 'Looking at the President's body, you couldn't say exactly where he was hit—too much damage.'

The Doctor shuddered at this rather gruesome piece of professional expertise. Still, at least they'd found the mark. One more piece of evidence to support his story.

Runcible finally unscrewed the heavy drum-lid and peered inside. His face twisted, and he screamed ...

Far below the Doctor and the others heard the scream.

The note of pure terror in the voice sent them running for the staircase.

Runcible lay huddled at the foot of the camera. He had fainted from sheer fright. Beside him, a black-cowled figure was rapidly sorting through the cassettes inside the drum.

There came a sound of running feet, and Spandrell's voice echoed down the service gallery. 'Runcible, where are you? Are you all right?' With a hiss of anger, the figure slipped away into the darkness.

A few minutes later, Spandrell appeared, the Doctor and Hildred close behind. He knelt beside Runcible's body, and the little commentator stirred, and gave a feeble moan.

'He's alive anyway,' said the Doctor. 'What happened, Runcible?'

'Horrible,' moaned Runcible. 'It's *horrible* ...'

'What happened?' demanded Spandrell.

Runcible struggled to sit up. 'My technician. He's in there—in the drum ...'

In one long stride the Doctor crossed to the camera and peered inside the drum. Spandrell looked over his shoulder.

Stuffed inside the drum was a tiny, twisted corpse.

6

Into the Matrix

Spandrell looked at the Doctor in baffled horror. 'What's happened to him?'

'Matter condensation,' said the Doctor briefly. 'It's a particularly revolting death.'

'No wonder we couldn't find him,' said Spandrell, and turned away in distaste. 'I've never seen anything like it.'

'I have, I'm afraid,' said the Doctor softly.

'You have? Where?'

'It's an unpleasant technique the Master acquired, somewhere on his travels. You might say it's a kind of trademark.'

'And who is the Master?'

'Who is the Master?' The Doctor swung round to face him. 'My sworn enemy, Castellan Spandrell. A fiend who glories in chaos and destruction. If he's back on Gallifrey ...'

'Back?' Spandrell pounced on the word. 'You mean he's a Time Lord?'

'He was—a long while ago. You know, a lot of things are suddenly becoming clearer.'

Spandrell gave him a long-suffering look. 'Not to me, they're not.'

'If the Master *is* here, this must be his final

challenge.' He gestured towards the technician's body. 'And *that* is just a sort of greetings card. A little joke.'

Spandrell wondered what kind of twisted mind could find humour in a shrunken corpse. 'Take that thing away, Hildred,' he ordered. 'First take the video cassettes out and give them to Commentator Runcible. Runcible, you find the one we need.'

Runcible took the cassettes from Hildred and Hildred screwed the lid back on the drum, and lifted it from the camera.

Runcible fumbled through the cassettes with shaking hands, while Spandrell watched him sourly. 'Well, have you found what we want?'

'This is the one, Castellan. You can tell by the numbers.'

'*I* can tell when I see it, and not before. Take it down to Records, I'll look at it there.'

'Right, Castellan.' Runcible took the cassette, climbed unsteadily to his feet and set off down the gallery.

Spandrell turned to the Doctor, 'I shall want to know everything you can tell me about this Master. And I warn you now, if there's some kind of private feud between you—don't try to settle it on Gallifrey.'

The Doctor was unimpressed by the threat in Spandrell's voice.

'It can't be avoided, Castellan,' he said sombrely. 'Like it or not, Gallifrey is involved. And it may never be the same again. Let me tell you a little about the Master . . .'

As they walked along the darkened service gallery

and down the stairs, the Doctor gave Spandrell a brief summary of the Master's evil career.

'Mind you,' he concluded, 'that isn't the whole story by any means. I lost sight of the Master on Earth some time ago. There's no telling what he's been up to since then.'

Spandrell grunted. 'If he is, or was, a Time Lord, there'll be some kind of data extract in the files ...'

'Perhaps,' said the Doctor thoughtfully.

'What do you mean, perhaps?' grumbled Spandrell. 'A full biography is kept on every ...' He broke off as a small, plump figure came towards them. 'Runcible? What's the matter?'

Runcible stumbled slowly forward, his empty hands held out, as if in apology. 'The cassette ... Somebody ... some——' He fell forward onto his face. From between his shoulder-blades projected the handle of a knife.

'Four cold-blooded killings in one day!' said Spandrell explosively. Too restless to sit down, he strode up and down between the data banks of the Record Section.

Sprawled in Engin's favourite chair, the Doctor seemed totally relaxed. 'Fleabites, Spandrell,' he said with gloomy relish. 'We've hardly started yet. Things will get worse before they get better.'

'Here—in the Capitol?' Spandrell was appalled.

'Well, perhaps it will shake a few Time Lords out of their lethargy. They live for centuries and they have as much sense of adventure as dormice!'

Looking very like an old white dormouse himself,

Co-ordinator Engin came scurrying between his data banks. 'I'm afraid there's nothing, Castellan. No record of any Time Lord who ever adopted the title of "Master".'

'Told you,' said the Doctor unrepentantly. 'If there was a data extract on the Master, destroying it would be his first move.'

'Indeed? Yet the Co-ordinator here assures me that Time Lords Data extracts cannot be withdrawn, without the fact being recorded. I thought someone had scanned *your* extract, Doctor, but apparently that's impossible.'

'Rubbish,' said the Doctor vigorously. 'Simple for anyone with a little criminal know-how. Even I could do it.'

Engin cackled disbelievingly. 'You would need more than *criminal* know-how, Doctor. Advanced exitonic circuitry of this kind ...'

The Doctor jumped to his feet. 'Child's play to the Master. You think this is a sophisticated system?' The Doctor waved a dismissive hand at the rows of data banks. 'There are planets out there where this sort of thing would be considered prehistoric.'

The Doctor's attack on his beloved Records Section made old Engin splutter with rage. 'Of all the arrogant, unmitigated rubbish ...'.

Hurriedly Spandrell asked the Doctor, 'What's the Master like on mathematics?'

The Doctor was prowling restlessly about the Record Section as if searching for some clue. 'Absolutely brilliant. Almost up to my standard.' He paused before a corner area where complex data banks surrounded a low couch. The couch itself seemed to be wired into a nearby console. 'What's all this?' he demanded.

Engin hobbled over. 'One of our prehistoric pieces of equipment,' he said acidly. 'It's the A.P.C. Section.'

'A.P.C.?'

'Amplified Panotropic Computations.'

The Doctor nodded. 'In other words—brain cells!'

Engin fixed him with a reproving eye. 'Trillions of electro-chemical cells in a continuous matrix, a master-pattern. At the moment of death an electrical scan is made of the brain pattern and these millions of impulses are immediately transferred ...'

'Yes, yes, the theory's simple enough,' said the Doctor impatiently. 'What's the function?'

'The Matrix is a huge communal brain. It monitors the life of the Capitol, and makes provision for the future. We use its accumulated wisdom and experience to predict future events and to plan how to deal with them.'

'What about the assassination of the President?'

'For some reason that was not foreseen,' said the old Co-ordinator sadly.

The Doctor was suddenly jubilant. 'Oh yes it was, my dear old Engin. It was foreseen by *me*! Oh that's very clever. He's really surpassed himself this time!'

Spandrell was beginning to lose patience. 'What *are* you talking about, Doctor?'

'Don't you see? Time Lords are telepathic, and this thing here is a very complex brain. The Master intercepted its forecast of the assassination and beamed it into my mind.'

Spandrell was bemused. 'Is that even possible?'

'Yes,' said the Doctor, positively. 'Yes, the Master could do it. Spandrell, you say you thought my data extract had been scanned?'

'Yes. There was no mica-dust.'

'He'd need my biography print to beam a message accurately over such a distance ... it all hangs together, Spandrell.'

'Maybe. Why would the Master want you to know his plan?'

'I told you. He's got a lot of old scores to settle.'

Engin was still unconvinced. 'Doctor, I simply do not believe that anyone could do what you are suggesting. How can one intercept thought-patterns within the Matrix itself?'

'By going in there—joining it?'

'A living mind?' asked Spandrell incredulously.

'Why not? In a sense that's all a living mind is— electro-chemical impulses.' The Doctor paused. 'And if I went in there myself I could track him down and destroy him ...'

Engin shook his head. 'I couldn't allow it. The psychosomatic feedback might very well kill you. The thing's never been done before ... far too dangerous.'

'It's better than being vaporised, Co-ordinator. That's what's waiting for me if I don't go in.'

Engin looked worriedly at Spandrell. The Castellan nodded. 'Let him try it. He's got very little to lose.'

Engin remained dubious, but at last they managed to persuade him. 'Very well,' he sighed. 'If you'll lie down on the couch, Doctor.'

The Doctor stretched out, and Engin began applying a variety of electrodes to his head and body. 'Is this what happens to the near-deceased?' asked the Doctor cheerfully.

Engin gave a rather embarrassed cough. 'Well yes —though they are normally unconscious. This will be a considerable shock to your system, Doctor. There may be some pain ...'

The Doctor braced himself. 'I'm ready when you are.'

Engin still hesitated. 'You're *sure* you want to do this?'

The Doctor didn't want to do it in the least, but he could see no alternative. 'Oh get on with it!'

Engin threw a switch, and the Doctor's body arched as though electrocuted. For a moment his entire body was bent like a bow. Then it slumped back onto the couch, the breathing so shallow that it was almost undetectable.

Spandrell leaned over the couch in alarm. 'What's happening to him?'

Engin studied the row of dials on the console before him. 'Well, apparently it worked, Castellan. Only the Doctor's body is with us now. His mind has gone into the Matrix.'

The Doctor was lying against a rock in the middle of an enormous plain. From all around came booming, mad laughter, filling the skies like thunder.

He struggled to his feet and took a step forward. All at once there was a river before him. Out surged a giant crocodile, jaws gaping wide. The Doctor jumped back, his foot twisting beneath him—and tumbled over the edge of a precipice. He scrabbled for a hold, grabbing desperately at a projecting root. For a moment he hung over a colossal drop, the endless mad laughter booming in his ears.

Holding on with one hand, the Doctor whipped the scarf from his neck and looped it round an overhanging tree. Grabbing both ends, he started hauling himself up.

A terrifying figure appeared on the cliff-top above him. Robed and masked, it carried an enormous sword. With no particular surprise, the Doctor recognised a Japanese Samurai warrior from the planet Earth.

The sword swept down cutting through the scarf, and the Doctor fell into endless space ...

7

Death by Terror

The Doctor's body lay motionless on the couch. Spandrell looked on helplessly, while Engin studied a monitor panel. Suddenly a steadily pulsing blip of light on the central gauge faded to nothingness. 'It's stopped,' said Engin sadly.

'What's stopped?'

'Brain activity.' Engin showed Spandrell the dial. 'Look, there's nothing registering.'

'Does that mean he's dead?'

The old Co-ordinator shrugged. 'Virtually. I warned him. The psychic shock of that environment ...'

Spandrell leaned over the Doctor's body. 'But he's still breathing—just about.'

Engin nodded. 'Motor activity. Often continues for some little time ... No, wait a minute ...' The blip had picked up. It was pulsing brightly. 'He's back! His brain must have an unusually high level of artron energy.'

The Doctor's chest was rising and falling, as his breathing became more regular. Spandrell looked down at him. 'What do you think's happening?'

Engin scanned his monitor dials. 'I don't know, Castellan. But whatever it is—to the Doctor it's completely and utterly real—real enough to kill him. If he dies in there—he'll die here too.'

The Doctor opened his eyes. He was stretched out on an operating table. Above him loomed the masked, gowned figure of a surgeon. There must have been an accident, thought the Doctor muzzily. He'd been hurt, and now he was in hospital. Yet there was something terribly wrong. Why was the operating table set up in the middle of an open plain? And why was the surgeon lunging at him with an enormous hypodermic?

'You were a fool, Doctor, to enter my domain,' shouted the surgeon.

In sudden panic, the Doctor rolled from the table. He hit hard, rocky ground, scrambled to his feet and started running ...

He was on a battlefield, shells whistling all around him. A battle-weary soldier on an equally weary horse appeared out of the smoke and plodded towards him. Grotesquely, both soldier and horse were wearing gas masks. There was something sinister about them, a smell of death. The Doctor turned and fled ...

He was running along a railway track. A masked guard loomed up before him, and pulled a heavy lever. The lines at the Doctor's feet shifted, as the points were changed. His foot was trapped between the rails. There was an express train roaring along the line towards him ...

'No,' shouted the Doctor. 'No!' His foot came free —and the train roared past ...

... and he was stumbling over rocky ground. There was a sudden splintering crack. The Doctor looked down. He had stepped onto an enormous green egg. The case was shattered, and green liquid dripped from his foot. Somewhere in the distance there was a sniggering sound, like an evil child.

The Doctor made a mighty effort to concentrate his mind. He knew well enough what was happening to him. His adversary was attacking while he was still off-balance, trying to destroy him with all the traditional terrors—falling, illness, war, being trapped ... Unless the Doctor started fighting back, his enemy would hunt him down and kill him. Mental death, death by terror here in the Matrix, would mean physical death for the helpless body on the couch.

The Doctor stared hard at the plain around him. 'I deny this reality ... the true reality is a computation Matrix.'

The scene before him blurred—and turned into an endless vista of condensers and giant solid-state circuits. The Doctor knew his brain was perceiving the true nature of the Matrix that held it ... But the effort was too great, his enemy's reality too well established. The picture faded ...

This time he was at the bottom of a rocky quarry. It was unbearably hot. A vulture wheeled overhead in the coppery sky.

Doggedly the Doctor scrambled to his feet. He was

very thirsty, and he could hear water trickling ... It seemed to come from beneath a patch of damp sand. A hidden spring, perhaps ... The Doctor scraped away the sand to reveal not water, but a shining mirror. A clown's face leered up at him, and burst into a wild howl of laughter ... The vision faded, and the Doctor looked round; he was alone in the quarry. A voice boomed, '*I* am the creator here, Doctor. This is my world. There is no escape for you!' There was something oddly familiar about that voice, thought the Doctor, distorted though it was. He started climbing out of the quarry.

He was trudging across a dusty plain, beneath an ever-burning sun. Just ahead was a range of jungle-covered hills, with occasional outcrops of bare rock. There was a drone high above him. The Doctor looked up. An old-fashioned biplane was circling overhead. As the Doctor watched, the plane banked steeply, and dived straight towards him. He turned and ran. There was a staccato chattering and machine-gun bullets sprayed all round him. The Doctor saw a rocky gully and dived for it, rolling over and over, bullets tearing up the ground. His left leg felt suddenly numb ... The Doctor looked up. The plane was so low now that he could see the helmeted, goggled face of the pilot, laughing in triumph. The plane rose slowly and disappeared into the sky.

The Doctor looked at his leg. It was twisted at an awkward angle, and blood was seeping slowly through the cloth. 'I deny this reality,' he shouted. 'I deny it.'

The blood disappeared and his leg was whole again.

The voice from nowhere howled, 'You are trapped in my creation—and *my* reality rules here.'

The Doctor looked down. His leg was bleeding once more. 'All right,' muttered the Doctor grimly. 'Then I'll fight you in your reality—and on your own terms.' He tore a strip from his shirt and started bandaging his leg.

'It will be my pleasure to destroy you, Doctor,' threatened the voice. 'Be on guard!'

Engin studied his monitoring panel. The Doctor lay quite still on his couch, electrodes clamped to his head.

'His pulse has increased,' said Engin slowly. 'And there's a massive blood sugar demand.'

'What does that mean?'

'He's preparing to run—or to fight.'

'Then in that case,' asked Spandrell, '*who*, or *what*, is he fighting?'

'Presumably—another hostile mind.'

In the hidden chamber deep beneath the Capitol another A.P.C. set-up had been installed, secretly linked by the Master to the power-lines that fed the Matrix. The Time Lord who was now the Master's servant lay prone on a couch. The Master's bodily degeneration was too far advanced for him to undergo the physical strain involved in entering the Matrix. In any case, he had always preferred to find others to endure such risks. So it was the Time Lord whose mind was now inside the Matrix, the Time Lord who was risking life and sanity in an attempt to destroy the Doctor.

There was a flat plastic disc covering the Time Lord's face. It showed the Master what his servant was seeing, in the phantom world of the Matrix. At the moment it was little enough—a vista of heavy jungle, as the Time Lord's Matrix-self forced its way through the undergrowth.

The Master seemed well-satisfied. 'We have him now,' he hissed. 'But be wary. The Doctor is never more dangerous than when the odds are against him.'

A Chancellery Guard stood motionless in the corner. But his staring eyes saw nothing. He was under the Master's control, a mindless tool waiting to be used.

The Doctor finished bandaging his leg, and stood up to see if it would bear his weight. The leg was painful, and stiffening rapidly, but he could still walk. Ignoring the discomfort, he moved out of the rocks, and headed for the cover of the nearby jungle.

As soon as the Doctor was out of sight, the Hunter appeared. He wore dark jungle-green clothing, and his face was obscured by a jungle hat to which was fastened a camouflage net. He carried an elaborate telescopically-sighted rifle. His belt held a holstered pistol and a heavy knife. More equipment was packed into the light haversack on his back. Perfectly trained, fully equipped for jungle warfare, he was a formidable and terrifying figure.

Lightweight binoculars were slung round his neck,

and he was using them to scan the jungle ahead. Soon he froze, smiling in satisfaction. In the vision-field of the binoculars he could see the Doctor, working his way painfully up a rocky slope. The Doctor's trousers were torn, and his shirt was a tattered rag. He was tired, hungry and thirsty—and wounded. Above all, he was lost and confused in a world not of his making. The Hunter smiled. It wouldn't take long to finish so weak an opponent. He raised his rifle to his shoulder.

The Doctor had just paused for a much-needed rest when an explosive bullet blew a chunk from the rock beside his head. He rolled over and ran desperately for cover.

Scrambling to his feet, the Doctor burst through a dense clump of bushes, crossed a shallow valley and started climbing yet another rocky hill. Bullets buzzed about him like angry wasps. The Doctor reached the top of the hill and began a wild scramble down the other side. For the moment the hill itself shielded him from his pursuer. He looked round for a hiding place, and spotted a shallow cave. Scrambling inside, he pulled vegetation over the entrance to conceal himself, and crouched waiting.

From the back of the cave an enormous purple spider watched him from its web.

Belly-down on the ground, the Hunter crawled over the skyline, fearing that the Doctor would be waiting in ambush. Seeing nothing, he rose to his feet, and began descending the other side, rifle at the ready.

The Doctor crouched motionless in his cave as the booted feet came ever nearer.

The Hunter was only a few feet away from the

Doctor's hiding place. He looked round suspiciously, sensing that the Doctor was near, but unable to see him. He took the water bottle from his pack, and drank thirstily—and the act of drinking gave him an idea. 'That's it,' he whispered to himself. 'He'll need water soon. He'll have to come to water.'

Light as it was, the pack was slowing his movements. Slipping it from his shoulders, he hid it beneath a bush, then moved quietly away into the jungle.

A few minutes later, the Doctor crept out from his cave. He listened cautiously for a moment, then dragged out the Hunter's pack and started rummaging through it. Opening the water-bottle he lifted it eagerly to his lips—it was empty. He tossed it aside and started searching the pack. He found spare magazines, night-sights, plastic explosive, electric detonators, field rations, even a hand-grenade. 'Everything but an anti-tank gun,' muttered the Doctor morosely. He hefted the hand-grenade thoughtfully for a moment. Then he searched through the pack again, until he found a coil of very fine wire.

The Doctor chose a tree just beyond the bush, and higher up the hill. Carefully, he wedged the hand-grenade into the fork of one of its branches. He tied the wire round the pin of the grenade, then, unwinding the wire coil behind him, he moved back to the bush. Hurriedly re-packing the Hunter's haversack, he fastened the other end of the wire to a buckle, leaving just enough slack to allow him to thrust the knapsack back under the bush. Kicking dust and twigs over the length of the wire between bush and tree, the Doctor limped away into the jungle. The Hunter crouched by a jungle water hole, took a phial from his pocket and tipped it into the pool. An ugly green stain spread slowly over the surface of the water, gradually disappearing as the liquid dissolved. Tossing the phial to one side, the Hunter moved quietly away.

The Doctor came limping along the track, searching the jungle in his quest for water. Suddenly he paused. He could hear rustling. Then he relaxed—the sound was moving away from him. 'Wonder what he's been up to,' he thought, and moved cautiously on.

The Hunter ran back through the jungle to the place where he had left his haversack. He soon found the right bush, but the haversack seemed to be jammed. He tugged at it impatiently ...

The Hunter's tugging tightened the wire, which pulled the pin from the grenade, at the same time dislodging it from its tree-fork ...

Puzzled, the Hunter looked down at the haversack, and saw the wire fastened to the buckle. Immediately suspecting a trap he jumped to his feet—just in time to see the grenade rolling downhill towards him ...

With a shout of alarm the Hunter threw himself to one side, rolling over and over. The grenade exploded in a shattering blast of flame and smoke. Dust filled the air, and rock fragments rained down into the surrounding jungle.

Not far away, the Doctor was resting wearily against a tree. He lifted his head eagerly at the sound of the explosion, and as its echoes died away, he gazed hopefully around him. He saw only the familiar vista of hills and jungle. His head sunk despondently on his chest. 'Didn't get him after all ... if I had this nightmare would have vanished.' Rocks and jungle were only the creation of his enemy's mind. And since they were still here, his enemy still lived.

The Hunter picked himself up. He was dazed, dusty and wounded. Blood welled slowly from a gash in his side. Beneath the camouflage mask, his face was twisted in hate. 'A good try, Doctor. But not quite good enough!' Painfully he wriggled round, reached into his pack for an emergency dressing. He ripped open his jacket and started to bandage his wounds.

The Master straightened up with an angry snarl. 'The fool! To let himself be booby-trapped like that—the psychic shock might well have been fatal.' He studied the readings on his monitor dials. 'Physical condition worsening. If he doesn't finish the Doctor off soon ... he'll lose.'

The Master limped angrily about the room, cursing his physical deterioration. The trouble with working through others was that you were powerless to correct their bungling. He remembered the Guard sitting in the corner of the room, and came to a halt in front of him. A skeletal finger reached out to touch the Guard's forehead. 'Stand!'

The Guard rose and stood to attention, eyes glazed

and face blank. 'I have a task for you,' whispered the Master. 'There may be difficulties. Others may seek to prevent you from carrying out my orders. You will ignore them, and obey only me. You will let nothing stop you, do you understand?'

The Guard's voice was flat and emotionless. 'Yes, Master. I will obey only you.'

'Then this is what you must do ...' Hoarsely the Master gave a series of commands. The Guard marched away.

The Master's bloodless lips drew back in a smile of hatred. The body, as well as the mind, could be attacked. If the Master's plan worked, the struggle within the Matrix would soon be ended—by the Doctor's death ...

8

Duel to the Death

The Doctor broke into a shambling run at the sight of the water hole. He was very thirsty now, and the little pool of cool clear water seemed like some wonderful mirage. But it was real enough—as real as anything was here ... The Doctor flung himself down, cupped his hands in the water and started to drink.

His lips were actually touching the water, when he saw the dead fish floating just below the surface of the pool. He paused, letting the water drain away between his hands, and looked deeper into the pool. There was another dead fish—and another.

Slowly the Doctor straightened up, forcing himself to move away from the water. He began a methodical search of the area around the pool. Before very long, he discovered the phial the Hunter had thrown away. The Doctor took off the stopper and sniffed cautiously. There were still a few drops of oily green liquid left in the bottom. He stoppered the phial and slipped it into his pocket. Perhaps he could find a way to turn the enemy's weapon against him ...

There was a clump of bamboo growing near the pool, and an idea came to him. He broke off first a fairly thick bamboo cane and then a very thin one. He found a flat rock and started digging a shallow

81

hole beside the little pool. When the hole was finished, the Doctor began using the thin cane to push the soft pith from the centre of the thick one. He worked with frantic speed. The Hunter couldn't be very far away.

By now the Hunter had finished dressing his wounds. He climbed stiffly to his feet, picked up his rifle and started moving back towards the water hole ...

A few inches of water had seeped into the bottom of the Doctor's hole. It came from the underground spring that fed the water hole itself—pure water un-contaminated by the Hunter's poison. Unable to wait any longer, the Doctor dipped his hollowed-out bamboo cane into the inch or two of muddy water and sucked greedily. Soon the water was gone. Some instinct told the Doctor there was no time to wait for more. He got to his feet, still clutching the bamboo cane, and moved off into the jungle.

The Hunter limped down the path to the water hole, rifle at the ready. He stood by the pool a moment, reading the Doctor's movements from his tracks. He saw the newly-dug mud-hole, and smiled. Water was only just seeping into the bottom again—which meant the Doctor wasn't far away.

He raised his voice in a taunting shout, 'I'm very close to you now, Doctor. You'd better start running ...'

The Doctor was already running, forcing his way through the jungle. At the sound of the Hunter's voice he increased his pace—and blundered straight into a clump of thorn-trees. He tried to tear himself free but the thorns were long and sharp, tearing savagely at his clothing, and at his flesh.

The Hunter heard the crackling, smiled in satisfaction, and set off at a run.

The Doctor forced himself to move slowly and patiently, unhooking the tangling thorns one by one. As the last thorn came free, he could hear the Hunter crashing through the jungle.

The Doctor looked round wildly, and a desperate plan formed in his mind. He snapped off several of the longest thorns, and headed for a huge gnarled tree that grew nearby. Bamboo cane in one hand, he grabbed one of the lower branches and began hauling himself painfully upwards, handicapped by his tiredness, and the pain from his wounded leg.

Finally he reached his objective, a broad high branch which overhung the jungle floor. Sprawled on top of it, the Doctor fished out the phial and one of the thorns. He dipped the point of the thorn into the drops of green liquid in the phial. Then he slipped the treated thorn into one end of his hollow bamboo cane—and waited.

The Hunter appeared below him, limping stiffly through the jungle. Like the Doctor, he was ragged and exhausted. But it was clear from the way he held the high-powered rifle that every sense was on the alert.

The Doctor watched him pass beneath the tree,

raised his improvised blow-pipe to his lips and *blew*.

The second he felt the sting of the thorn the Hunter whirled round and fired. Shot like a roosting bird, the Doctor tumbled from his tree and crashed down into the undergrowth. clutching his arm.

The Hunter moved to finish him off—and became aware of a spreading numbness ... He looked down and saw the thorn projecting from his thigh. Gritting his teeth he plucked it out. His face paled at the sight of the green stain on its tip. He had minutes to live—unless ...

Throwing the thorn aside, he began hunting frantically through his pockets. With a sigh of relief, he found a pocket medi-kit, opened the little case and took out an injector-phial of antidote. Quickly he plunged the injector-needle into the muscle above the wound.

The Doctor staggered to his feet, his wounded arm hanging limply by his side. He looked round at the absorbed Hunter and realised he had only a few moments to escape. Gathering the remnants of his strength, the Doctor reeled off into the cover of the jungle.

A Chancellery Guard marched stiffly into the Records Section and came to attention before Spandrell.

'Message from the Chancellor, sir. He wants the Doctor brought to him for interrogation.'

'You're Solis, aren't you? One of the Chancellor's personal bodyguard.'

'That's right, sir.'

'Well, whoever he is, he will have to wait,' said Engin peevishly. 'I can't just snatch the Doctor's mind out of the Matrix. The shock would kill him.'

'You mean we can't get him out?' asked Spandrell. 'What *do* we do then?'

'Wait till he comes back of his own accord—*if* he does. When the mind is back in the body, the body can be disconnected from the machine—and not before.'

Spandrell waved the Guard to one side. 'You heard the Co-ordinator. The Chancellor can't interrogate a corpse. You'll have to wait.'

Solis nodded silently, and took up a position close to the monitor console.

Spandrell turned back to Engin. 'How long can a living mind exist in there?'

'I've no idea. There's just no data available. But I can tell you this—his body's on the point of collapse.' Engin pointed towards the monitor console. 'Low blood pressure, shallow respiration ... He can't go on much longer.'

Solis was studying the area around the couch. The various electrodes connecting the Doctor to the machine all came together at one main point. If those wires were wrenched free, the Doctor would die from the shock—and Solis would have carried out his mission.

Very slowly he began edging nearer to the console.

The Doctor staggered on through the jungle, too weak to think of fighting. The one idea in his mind was to survive. Somehow he must outlast his terrible enemy. 'Must keep going,' he muttered. 'I *must* keep going.'

He stumbled and fell, and lay gasping, feeling as if he could never move again. Then he struggled slowly to his feet and staggered on. '*I must keep going...*'

Ahead of him the jungle was thinning out. Beyond it there was a misty swamp bordering a stagnant palm-fringed lagoon. The Doctor stumbled on towards the water.

Following close behind, the Hunter was almost as exhausted as his quarry. His side throbbed dully, and even after the antidote, the poisoned thorn had left his right leg feeling numb and heavy. But like the Doctor, he was utterly determined not to give up.

He reached the spot where the Doctor had fallen, and examined the place where the Doctor's body had rested. The Hunter fingered a blade of blood-stained grass. 'He can't last much longer,' he muttered. 'He *can't*.' The hoarse whisper was almost a prayer. The Hunter knew he couldn't last much longer himself.

'It's only a *mental* battle they're fighting,' said Spandrell angrily. 'If the Doctor is losing, why doesn't he just pull out?'

'It isn't that simple. His adversary must have been in the Matrix many times before. He's created a kind of mental landscape—a *dreamscape* if you like. The Doctor's caught up in it ...' Engin noticed a flicker of movement beside him, and turned to see Solis stretching a hand towards the nexus of electrode wires.

'Don't touch, you fool! Do you want to kill him?'

'Sorry sir. Just curious.' Solis moved back—but not very far.

'If the Doctor is trapped in his enemy's world,' insisted Spandrell, 'then the enemy is bound to be stronger. The Doctor doesn't stand a chance.'

'Well, perhaps a very slight one.' Engin looked up from the monitor dials. 'You see, Castellan, the Doctor's opponent is expending energy in the very act of maintaining the reality-projection he has created. The Doctor, on the other hand, is free to employ all his mental energy for self-defence.'

Solis had edged closer by now. He stretched out a stealthy hand towards the clump of wires. By the time Spandrell registered the stealthy movement, it was almost too late. 'Get back,' he roared. 'Get back!'

Solis lunged forward. As his finger-tips touched the wires Spandrell drew his staser and fired all in one smooth motion. Solis was hurled back by the massive shock of the staser-bolt. He should have collapsed at once but so strong was the Master's hypnotic command that the dying body lurched forward in an attempt to carry out its mission. Horrified, Spandrell fired again, and again, and the body jerked and lay still.

Slowly, Spandrell holstered his staser as frightened attendants came running from all sides. Engin looked at the Doctor, stretched immobile on the couch, then studied the monitor dials. 'He's calling on all his reserves,' he whispered. 'The final struggle is about to begin!'

Entering the marsh had been a bad mistake, thought

the Doctor. True he had been able to drink from the lagoon, and the brackish water had made him feel stronger. But the ground was soft and boggy now and progress was very slow. He pulled a long straight branch from a fallen tree, stripped it into a staff and used it to feel his way along. He had no wish to be trapped sinking in a swamp when the Hunter caught up with him. Would his enemy haul him out for the pleasure of shooting him, wondered the Doctor? Or would he simply sit and watch him disappear slowly beneath the mud?

Just ahead of him was an area of scattered shallow mud-pools. From time to time one or another of them produced a sudden pop. 'Marsh gas,' thought the Doctor. He sniffed. 'Smells like methane ...'

Just beyond the pools was a clump of bushes. The Doctor limped slowly towards it. He burrowed deep beneath the shelter of the broad leaves and slid forward onto his face, head pillowed in his arms. The loss of blood from his wounds, and the arduous journey through jungle and swamp had been too much for him. He was utterly exhausted.

So too was the Hunter. He was lurching wearily through the swamp, stumbling blindly on, his eyes glazed with fatigue. The swampy landscape seemed to dissolve and swim about him, as if the world of his creation was about to disappear.

The Hunter's exhaustion was registered on the

monitor panels in the underground chamber where his real, physical body still lay. The Master hovered angrily over the unconscious form of his champion. 'Come, one final effort. Kill the Doctor. Destroy him. I, the Master, command you!'

The Hunter straightened up, like a puppet when its operator tightens the strings. Once more, fresh and alert, he gazed keenly round the swamps and picked up the clear tracks leading to the Doctor's hiding place.

Picking his way towards the bubbling pools, he shouted, 'Where are you, Doctor? You can't win now— you might as well give up!'

Wearily the Doctor raised his head. Parting the leaves, he saw the Hunter advancing towards him, rifle at the ready.

The Doctor wriggled backwards, into deeper cover. 'What do you want?'

The Hunter's voice rang back. 'Only your life, Doctor ...' There was a peal of hideous laughter. 'Only your life, for my Master!'

'I'll make a bargain with you!'

'No bargains. Show yourself, Doctor. Get it over with. Do you hear me?'

The Doctor was working his way to the far edge of the clump of swamp-bushes. 'No!' he shouted. 'You show yourself, first. Your *real* self.'

'Very well, Doctor.' The Hunter snatched off his mask and for the first time the Doctor saw the face of his enemy. It was Chancellor Goth.

The Doctor sighed wearily. How like the Master to corrupt the highest and the noblest of the Time Lords to his evil purposes. 'All right, Goth,' he called. 'You win. I'm coming out.'

Holding his long pole by one énd he slid it along the ground to its full extent, until it lodged against a bush as far away from him as he could reach. Watching the mud-pools, the Doctor chose his moment, then shoved hard.

Goth saw the movement of the bushes, swung up his rifle and fired—just as the nearest pool sent up a puff of inflammable marsh-gas.

The explosive bullet touched off the marsh-gas, and flames sprang up all around. Suddenly Goth was trapped in a ring of fire. His clothes caught fire and with a roar of pain he flung down his rifle and dashed madly towards the lagoon.

As he got to his feet and came out of the bushes the Doctor was just in time to see Goth plunge into the water and disappear.

Retrieving his pole, the Doctor ran after him. He must finish his enemy while he was weak—then his nightmare world would be finished too.

By the time the Doctor reached the lagoon, Goth was nowhere in sight. The dark, stagnant water was completely still. The Doctor waded in waist-deep, probing the water with his pole. This world was still in existence—which meant that somewhere Goth was still alive.

The water behind him exploded in spray, as Goth surfaced with the savage fury of an attacking shark. The Doctor tried to turn, but Goth was too quick for him. Gripping him savagely round the neck, Goth bore the Doctor down and down until his head was beneath the water. The Doctor flailed and struggled, sending up great clouds of spray. But Goth had a grip of iron. He thrust the Doctor down and down until his head was under water.

The Doctor kicked and struggled for a moment longer. Then suddenly his body went limp ...

'You're finished, Doctor,' snarled Goth. 'Finished!'

9

The End of Evil

Goth held the Doctor under water a moment longer, then relaxed his grip on the limp body. Suddenly the Doctor came to life, catapulting up and backwards, knocking Goth off his feet. As Goth disappeared under the water the Doctor raised his long pole and speared downwards, pinning Goth's body to the muddy bed of the lagoon.

There was frantic kicking and thrashing and bubbling as Goth churned up the water in his efforts to escape. Grimly, the Doctor bore down on the pole, using the last vestiges of his strength to hold Goth under ...

... and Goth's body vanished. The lagoon itself vanished, and the swamps and jungles around it.

The Doctor saw an endless vista of solid-state circuitry stretching ahead of him. Pretending to risk his champion's death rather than his defeat, the Master had snatched Goth out of the Matrix.

On the couch Goth's body thrashed and convulsed. Angrily the Master slammed down switches on his control console. 'You weak fool! You craven-hearted, spineless poltroon, you let the Doctor trick you. You have failed me!'

'He was too strong for me, Master ... too much mental energy.'

The Master was busy at his console setting up new circuits. Goth, too weak to move, watched him with alarm. 'What are you doing, Master?'

'There's only one chance now. I must trap him in the Matrix forever. I shall overload the neuron fields...'

'No, Master, no!' screamed Goth. 'For pity's sake take off these connections. You'll kill me!'

The Master shook his head. It would be a long and complex job to disconnect Goth from the machine without harming him—and every second was precious. 'I've no time to waste on you,' he muttered, and pulled the switch. Goth's body arched in pain as the connections burned out. As the final blackness swallowed him, Goth saw the face of the Master staring down at him. It was the twisted, malformed face of a decaying corpse ...

A series of explosions shook Engin's console, and smoke poured from the burnt-out connections. Engin reached for the main power switch in panic, but Spandrell grabbed his arm. 'Co-ordinator, you can't. If you cut the power, the Doctor will die in there.'

'The circuits are going. If there's a fire in there the whole panoptric net will burn out. Thousands of brain patterns destroyed for ever.'

'They're not alive,' said Spandrell brutally. 'The Doctor is—I hope!'

The Doctor was fleeing across a darkening plain. The sky was blazing, and there were shattering explosions all around him. The ground erupted in flames, and the Doctor realised it was useless to run. He stared unafraid at the devastated landscape. 'I deny this reality,' he shouted. 'Goth has gone—and his world must vanish too!' There was another tremendous explosion. The Doctor vanished into a cloud of choking yellow smoke ...

... and woke coughing on the couch in the Records Section. 'Do you mind,' he murmured, 'this is a non-smoking compartment!' He realised he was rambling, opened his eyes, and saw Spandrell staring down at him.

Engin looked up from his monitor console. 'It's all right, Castellan,' he called. 'He's made it!' He threw the main switch to cut the power. Then he went over to the Doctor, and began to remove the electrodes.

The Master cursed, as a warning light on his own console blinked out. 'They've cut the power to the panotropic net! The Doctor must have eluded me.'

Goth stirred feebly on the couch, feeling life ebb from his burnt-out body. 'You fiend,' he whispered. 'Why did I ever believe in you ...' His head fell back.

The Master ignored him, his mind racing. He knew the Doctor would soon be on his track. His decaying body was too infirm to endure a long chase. He might not even reach his TARDIS. Were Spandrell's Guards to hunt him through the Capitol like a dying rat? No! Not while there was a better way. He took a gleaming hypodermic from beneath his robe, pushed back his sleeve, and plunged the needle into the vein of one skeletal arm.

Spandrell helped the Doctor to sit up. 'How do you feel?'

'Tired,' said the Doctor. 'Very, very tired.' He tried to stand and staggered a little.

Spandrell helped him to sit down again. 'You'd better rest, Doctor. You took a terrible beating in there.'

The Doctor grinned. 'You should see the other fellow. Where is he, by the way?'

'Where's who?'

'Goth! We've got to find him. He's your assassin, Spandrell. He's been acting as the Master's leg man.'

'Goth,' said Spandrell slowly. 'So that's why he was so keen to have you executed.'

The Doctor made a mighty effort, and actually managed to get onto his feet. 'Exactly. It was Goth, remember, who ordered my TARDIS to be transducted to the Capitol ... He knew very well I was still in it. He just wanted to make sure I was in the right place at the right time.'

The Doctor tried a few tentative steps, as he felt

his strength returning. 'Goth and the Master must have set up their own private link into the Matrix, so they can't be very far away. We can use the link to trace them.' He came to a stop in front of the bemused Engin. 'What's below us here?'

'Below the tower itself? Only service ducts...'

'And below them?'

'Well, a long way down there are vaults and tunnels dating back to the old time. They were never destroyed, simply built over ... There's an old map somewhere...'

Now almost himself again, the Doctor said impatiently, 'Fetch it! Come on, what are you waiting for?' He bustled Engin away. Spandrell lifted his communicator. If they were going to hunt for the Master, he wanted some Guards at his back. No one was going to turn him into a miniaturised corpse.

It didn't take very long to find the Master's secret hiding place. Using Engin's map, the Doctor worked out the most likely points for the Master to have tapped the Matrix power lines, and then checked them one by one.

The search led far below the city, along dank echoing stone corridors and into musty vaults disused for hundreds of years. At last they found what they were looking for—at the bottom of a long flight of time-worn steps, there was a tiny stone-walled chamber. As soon as the Doctor entered it, he knew their search was over.

In one corner was an incongruous clutter of technological equipment ... the Master's monitor console, the power cables linking it to the Matrix. Goth's unconscious body was slumped back on the couch, just barely breathing.

Dominating the little room was a high-backed stone chair. In it sat a cowled figure, motionless as a statue. The Doctor went slowly up to it, and pushed back the cowl.

Spandrell was close behind him, blaster in hand. He recoiled at the sight of the ravaged face beneath the hood. 'Is it him, Doctor?'

The Doctor nodded. 'Yes ... it's the Master.' The Master's head lolled backwards. The eyes in the skull-like face stared sightlessly at the ceiling. With some distaste, Spandrell felt for a pulse in the skinny wrist. There was nothing. He let go of the wrist with relief. 'He's dead, right enough.'

Engin was examining Goth. 'The Chancellor's still alive ... barely.'

They moved to the couch, and Spandrell looked down at Goth. 'Not for long though, by the looks of him.'

Engin was disconnecting terminals from the Chancellor's body. 'He seems to have taken the full blast of power from the Matrix.'

Goth opened his eyes and looked up at the Doctor. 'So, Doctor. You beat us in the end.'

'Goth,' said the Doctor sadly. 'Why did you do it?'

'I wanted *power* ...' whispered the dying voice.

'You would have been President ...'

'No ...' gasped Goth painfully. 'The retiring President told me ... wasn't going to name me his successor. Thought I was too ambitious ...'

'So you killed him.'

Goth gestured weakly towards the motionless figure in the chair.

'I killed for *him*. The Master ... part of his plan ... doomsday plan ...'

The Doctor leaned forward. '*What* plan, Goth?'

Goth paused for a moment, then spoke with a last tremendous effort. 'I discovered him in hiding, on Tersurus ... He was already dying. No more regenerations ... He promised me power ... made me bring him to Gallifrey, and hide him down here ...' Goth closed his eyes.

The Doctor said urgently. 'Goth, you've got to tell us ... what was this doomsday plan?'

Spandrell pulled him away. 'It's no use, Doctor. He's dead.'

The Doctor glared down angrily at the body. 'Typical politician—they'll never give you a straight answer to a straight question.'

Spandrell looked at him in astonishment. Then suddenly he understood. Beneath his flippant manner, the Doctor was very worried.

Some time later, they were all in the Chancellery, explaining the astonishing sequence of events to Cardinal Borusa. The sudden death of both President and Chancellor had left the old Cardinal as the leader of the High Council. He was quite prepared to take over both offices until the crisis was over.

Despite the lateness of the hour, Borusa was still

fresh and alert, and he listened keenly as Spandrell concluded his account of the Chancellor's death. 'Apparently the Master tried to trap the Doctor in the Matrix by overloading the neuron fields, leaving Chancellor Goth still connected to the circuit. The shock killed him.'

'And the Master's own death?'

Spandrell shrugged. 'You might almost say natural causes, sir. The body was extremely decayed. It's a wonder he stayed alive so long. One can only presume that he had come to the end of his regeneration cycle prematurely.'

Borusa frowned. 'I understood he was relatively young—not much older than the Doctor here.'

The Doctor was standing by the window, brooding over the lights of the Capitol City far below. 'He was always a criminal, sir, throughout all his lives. Constant pressure, constant danger. Accelerated regenerations used as disguise ... He was simply burnt out.'

Borusa nodded sombrely. Time Lord regeneration was a delicate and complex business. When something did go wrong with it, the results were often catastrophic.

The old Cardinal sat brooding behind the huge ornate desk that had once belonged to Goth. Suddenly he stood up. 'No!' he said decisively.

The Doctor gave him a puzzled look. 'No, what?'

'This wild story. It's unacceptable.'

'It happens to be the truth.'

'Then we must adjust the truth!'

'Adjust it, Cardinal?' Engin was shocked. 'In what way?'

'In a way that will maintain confidence in the Time Lords, and in their leadership. How many people have seen Goth and the Master since their deaths?'

Spandrell considered. 'Apart from those of us in this room? Just Hildred and the Guards.'

'We can rely on their silence.' Borusa thought for a moment. 'Castellan, you will see that the appearance of the Master's body is altered. We all know the effects of a staser-bolt. It will be a simple matter to char the body beyond recognition.'

'For what purpose, Cardinal?'

Borusa looked round the circle of puzzled faces. 'The official story will be that the Master arrived secretly on Gallifrey, and assassinated the President. Before he could escape, Chancellor Goth tracked him down and killed him, unfortunately perishing himself in an exchange of staser fire.' Borusa gave a wintry smile. 'Now, that's a much better story. I can believe that.'

Engin was appalled. 'After all that happened, you're going to make *Goth* into a hero?'

'The people need heroes, Co-ordinator. Sometimes it's even necessary to invent them. Good for public morale.'

'And what of the Doctor's part in all this?' asked Spandrell.

'Best forgotten,' said Borusa briskly. 'Naturally, Doctor, all charges against you will be dropped.'

The Doctor gave a mock bow. 'How very kind.'

'Providing, of course, that you leave Gallifrey at once.'

'Somehow, Cardinal, I have no desire to stay.'

'Good. Now, I believe you know something of the Master's past?'

'We did bump into each other from time to time.'

'Before you leave you will assist Co-ordinator Engin to compile a new biography of him—to replace the one that was stolen. It needn't be entirely accurate, of course.'

'Like Time Lord history?'

Borusa ignored the jibe. 'A few facts will give it verisimilitude, Co-ordinator. We cannot make the Master into a public enemy if we know nothing about him.'

Engin bowed his head. 'If that is your order, Cardinal, I can have a new biography prepared by morning.'

'I leave it to you. Later I think we must hold a thorough review of data security. We cannot have Time Lord data extracts simply vanishing from the records.'

Spandrell accepted the implied rebuke. 'I quite agree, sir. I'll see procedures are tightened up.'

'You'll attend to the, er, cosmetic treatment.'

'I'm sorry, Cardinal?'

'The alteration in the appearance of the Master's body,' said Borusa impatiently.

'I'll give orders immediately.'

'Excellent. I think that's all, gentlemen.' With a brief nod of farewell, Cardinal Borusa strode from the room.

A little sadly, the Doctor watched him go. 'Only in

mathematics will you find the truth,' he murmured
to himself.

Engin stared at him. 'What was that, Doctor?'

'Something Borusa used to say, during my time at
the Academy. Now he's trying to prove it.'

In accordance with Spandrell's orders, Hildred and
the Guards were searching the Master's hiding place.
One of them found an empty hypodermic under the
Master's chair. He passed it over to Hildred, whose
wrist-communicator bleeped as he took it. Spandrell's
face appeared in the tiny screen. 'Hildred? A little
job for you. Don't worry, it's well within your
capability.'

'Yes, Castellan.'

Spandrell hesitated. 'I'd better explain in person.
Come to the Chancellery.'

'Immediately, Castellan.'

Slipping the empty hypodermic into his pocket,
Hildred hurried from the room.

The black-robed body of the Master still sat upright
in its high-backed chair. One of the Guards looked at
it then turned away, with a shudder. The Master's
bloodless lips seemed to have frozen in the trace of a
smile...

10

The Doomsday Plan

The Doctor was comfortably sprawled in Engin's chair. The Co-ordinator himself sat at a nearby data terminal, attempting to feed details of the Master's disreputable career into the computer. He was getting very little help from the Doctor, who was gazing abstractedly into space.

'Now then, Doctor,' said Engin hopefully. 'What about the Master's *character*?'

'*Bad*,' said the Doctor.

Engin sighed. 'If you could possibly be a *little* more specific?'

'All right. Evil. Cunning. Resourceful. Determined. Technologically brilliant. Highly developed powers of extrasensory-perception. A remarkable hynotist ...' The Doctor broke off the list. 'You know, Engin, the more I think about him, the more unlikely it all becomes.'

'What does?'

'That the Master would meekly accept death. It's not his style.'

'Death is something we must all accept in time, Doctor,' said the old Time Lord gently.

'*Not the Master*. That must be why he came back here to Gallifrey. He had some plan.'

Obstinately Engin said. 'If the Master had triggered the end of his regeneration cycle, no plan could postpone his death.'

'You're certain of that? Surely in *theory* ...'

'In theory, perhaps, Doctor. But in practice, any attempt to *renew* the regeneration cycle would call for colossal amounts of energy.'

'How colossal?'

'Oh, say, about as much as we use to power the time travel facility. In other words the power of the whole of Gallifrey.' Engin smiled tolerantly, confident he'd disposed of the Doctor's nonsensical theory. 'Besides, why concern yourself further with the Master's evil schemes? He's dead now.'

'How do we know his doomsday plan isn't already under way? He may have had other servants as well as Goth. His evil scheme may be ticking away like a time bomb at this very moment.'

The Doctor jumped up and began pacing restlessly up and down. 'So then ... Something to do with energy, and something connected with Goth becoming President.' He swung round. 'What's so special about the President, Engin?'

'Nothing. He's simply a Time Lord, usually of senior rank, elected to a position of formal authority. He holds the ancient symbols of office, of course ...'

'Symbols? What symbols?'

'Relics from the Old Time. The Sash of Rassilon, the Great Key ...'

The Doctor stopped his pacing about, and dropped back into Engin's chair. 'Tell me about Rassilon, Co-ordinator.'

Engin brightened. Ancient History was a pet subject of his, and he was always glad of any opportunity to discuss it. 'Well, it's all recorded in the Book of Old Time. But there is a modern transgram of the text— that's much less difficult ...'

'Could I hear it?'

'You mean—*now*?'

'Now,' said the Doctor firmly.

Engin gave a resigned sigh, and got slowly to his feet. Suddenly he saw that the Doctor was sitting bolt upright, an expression of keen attention on his face. 'What is it, Doctor?'

'I can hear my hair curling,' said the Doctor solemnly, and grinned. 'Either I'm on the track of something—or it's going to rain!'

In a Chancellery office, Spandrell was giving Hildred instructions. 'Now have you got everything clear, Commander?'

'Yes, Castellan.'

Spandrell regarded him dubiously. 'You know why I chose you for this special mission, Commander Hildred?'

'No, Castellan.'

'Because the Master is already dead—which means that even you aren't likely to miss the target.'

'No, sir,' said Hildred patiently. He could see it was going to be a long time before Spandrell let him forget the way the Doctor had tricked him, when he'd first arrived on Gallifrey. Hildred saluted and turned to leave. Then he paused, taking the empty hypodermic from his pocket. 'Castellan, we found this ... under the Master's chair.'

Spandrell examined the hypodermic. 'Empty ... There'll probably be enough traces of the drug to analyse, though. Thank you, Commander. Report back to me when you've—restructured the Master.'

Co-ordinator Engin was happily lecturing the Doctor on his favourite subject. 'You see, Doctor, today we think of Rassilon as an almost mythical hero, the legendary founder of our Time Lord civilisation. But in his own time, he was regarded principally as a cosmic engineer. This of course was before we turned aside from the barren road of pure technology ...'

'That's very interesting,' said the Doctor patiently. 'Could we hear some more of the transgram, do you think?'

Engin adjusted controls on the playback console before him. 'Now let me see, this should be the area you're interested in ...' He touched a control, and a clear, melodic voice came from the console. 'And Rassilon journeyed into the black void with a great fleet. Within the Void no light would shine, and nothing of that outer nature could continue in being, save that which existed within the Sash of Rassilon.'

'A Black Hole,' muttered the Doctor excitedly. 'That's what it means—it must be!'

The melodic voice went on. 'Now Rassilon created the Eye of Harmony, which balances all things so that they neither flux nor wither nor change their state in any measure. And in this Eye, he sealed the energies of the Void with the Great Key, and caused the Eye of Harmony to be brought to Gallifrey ...'

'What is the Great Key, Engin? You mentioned it before.'

Engin switched off the transgram. 'It's just a plain black rod ... it looks like ebonite. The President carries it on certain ceremonial occasions, but its original function is a complete mystery.'

'Where is it kept, when it is not in use?'

'In the Panopticon. There's a special display section of relics from the Old Time.'

'And the Sash of Rassilon?'

'Oh, that stays with the President. The tradition is that it must always be in his possession. In fact it is the actual handing over of the Sash that signifies the transfer of the Presidency from one Time Lord to another ...'

The Doctor wasn't listening. 'Of course—that must be it. What a stupendous egotist.'

'Who?'

'The Master, of course. Don't you see? The Eye of Harmony is the inexhaustible energy source that powers all Gallifrey. It was that energy which made possible the first experiments in time travel. It's the whole source and foundation of Time Lord power, taken for granted for thousands of years ... and the Master planned to steal it. He'd have destroyed Gallifrey, the Time Lords, *everything*—just for the sake of his own survival!'

Spandrell came towards them, the Master's empty hypodermic in his hand. 'It seems that the Master didn't die of natural causes after all, Doctor. Apparently he killed himself.'

The Doctor frowned. 'That's even *less* like him.' He took the hypodermic, broke it open and sniffed delicately.

'I'd be careful, Doctor. Presumably it's some deadly poison!'

'Tricophenylaldehyde!' said the Doctor triumphantly.

Spandrell was none the wiser. 'It produces instant death, no doubt?'

'It produces the *appearance* of death. It's a neural inhibitor.'

'*What?*'

'He's fooled us, Spandrell. *The Master is still alive!*'

Spandrell looked at him in sudden dismay. 'I've just sent Hildred to blast the Master's body with a staser-bolt.'

'Where?'

'The Panopticon vault ...'

In a gloomy shadowed vault beneath the Panopticon, three bodies lay at rest on their marble biers. First the President, still in his ceremonial robes, the wide metallic links of the Sash of Rassilon draped across the dead chest. Next Goth, his handsome face cold and still. And finally the Master, still shrouded in black robe and cowl.

Feet rang on the flagstones and Commander Hildred came into the vault. He looked at the three still forms and shuddered. For all Spandrell's jest, it wasn't so easy to shoot a man who was already dead.

Bracing himself, Hildred crossed to the Master's bier. He drew and cocked his staser-pistol, holding it to the ghastly skull-like head. The Master's eyes opened. They blazed with malevolent hypnotic power, and Hildred found that he couldn't move. A skinny hand reached out and took him by the throat ...

As Hildred's body sank slowly to the stone floor, the Master sat up, swinging his legs from the marble slab. From beneath his robe he produced a squat, oddly-shaped gun ...

Spandrell, Engin and the Doctor hurried along the gloomy corridors of the Panopticon. The Doctor had a premonition that they were already too late ...

When the Master heard the sound of approaching footsteps, he moved away from the President's body wrapped himself in the black cloak, and stepped back into the shadows. Seconds later, Spandrell appeared in the doorway. Hildred was nowhere to be seen— and the bier which had held the Master was empty. Spandrell turned as the Doctor and Engin came up. 'We're too late, Doctor. He's gone.'

As Spandrell walked forward to the Master's bier, his foot struck something soft beneath it. He looked down, and saw the dead body of Hildred, shrunken to the size of a doll.

The Doctor looked down at the wizened corpse.

'The Master is consumed by hatred. It's his one great weakness.'

'Weakness, Doctor?' croaked a rasping voice. They turned to see the Master emerging from the shadows, Hildred's staser-pistol in his claw-like hand. 'That's where you're wrong. Hatred is strength.'

The Doctor said calmly, 'Not in your case. You'd delay an execution while you pulled the wings off a fly.'

'This time, I assure you, Doctor, the execution will not be delayed. *Don't!*' The Master's staser swung round to cover Spandrell, who had been edging a hand towards his pistol. 'I assure you, Castellan, I am not nearly so infirm as I look.' Spandrell stood very still, and the Master waved the staser at Engin. 'You! Bring the Sash of Rassilon.'

Engin looked at the Doctor. 'It appears you were right, Doctor.'

'Why else do you think I feigned death?' sneered the Master. 'When Goth failed me it was necessary to use more direct means. The Sash is wasted on a dead President, don't you think? *Bring it to me!*'

'Engin, don't do it,' said the Doctor quietly.

The ruined face turned towards him. 'I have suffered enough from your stupid interference in my designs, Doctor. Now we are coming to the end of our conflict and the victory is mine!'

'Why did you bring me here?' asked the Doctor quietly.

The Master smiled. 'As a scapegoat for the killing of the President, Doctor. Who else but you, so despicably good, so insufferably compassionate. I wanted you to die in shame and disgrace, destroyed by your own people, as I shall destroy them.'

Spandrell took advantage of the Master's speech to make his move. He sprang forward, snatching at his staser. Instantly, the Master shot him down. At the same time the Doctor sprang—and the Master scuttled quickly to one side and fired again. The Doctor's body joined Spandrell's on the ground. The staser swung round to cover Engin. 'Now—bring me the Sash, you old fool, or you'll get the same!'

Too terrified to refuse, Engin lifted the Sash from the body of the President, and handed it over. The Master snatched it, then hurried to the door of the vault. He looked back at the frightened Co-ordinator. 'Don't worry, I'm not going to kill you. Your friends aren't dead either—only stunned. I want you all to live long enough to see the end of this accursed planet —and for the Doctor to taste the full bitterness of his defeat.'

The Master slipped through the doorway, and an iron security shutter crashed down behind him. Engin heard a groaning sound. The Doctor was struggling to sit up. Spandrell too was beginning to stir.

With Engin's help, the Doctor struggled to his feet. 'The Sash? What happened to it?'

'I'm afraid it's gone, Doctor. What could I do? After all it's only of symbolic value.'

The Doctor groaned. 'Didn't you understand anything I was telling you? That Sash is a technological miracle, a device to enable the wearer to tap the power of the Eye of Harmony. All the Master needs now is the Great Key, and he can draw upon a force capable of obliterating this entire planet.'

Engin was stunned. 'You can't mean that, Doctor?'

'Of course I mean it! Don't you realise what Rassilon did—what the Eye of Harmony *is*? "That which balances all things", remember. It can only be one thing—the nucleus of a Black Hole.'

'But surely the Eye of Harmony is only a myth?'

'A myth? All the power of the Time Lords devolves from it.' Again the Doctor quoted from the transgram. ' "Neither flux nor wither nor change their state ..." Somehow Rassilon stabilised the elements of a Black Hole and set them in an eternally dynamic equation balanced against the mass of this planet. To get the energy he needs, the Master means to upset that balance by stealing the Eye. It will mean the end of Gallifrey, and it could set off an anti-matter chain reaction that will end hundreds of worlds.'

Spandrell climbed painfully to his feet. 'A very interesting exposition, Doctor. Now what are we going to do about it?'

The Doctor went to the shutter and heaved with all his strength. Spandrell and Engin tried to help— but the shutter was immovable. They were trapped in the vault. Trapped with a dead President and a dead Chancellor—and the Master was free.

11

The Final Battle

Black cloak almost invisible in the darkness of the Panopticon Museum, the Master crossed to the display case where the Great Key rested on its velvet cushion. Melting the lock with a blast from his staser-pistol, he lifted the glass dome and snatched up the gleaming black rod.

Swiftly he made his way into the main hall and up on to the platform. In the exact centre, he found a metal plate, worn smooth by the feet of generations of incurious Time Lords. The Master touched the plate with the black rod. It slid aside, to reveal a hole—the lock to which the black rod was the key. He slid the tip of the rod into the hole and turned it. There was a click, and a hum of power. There followed a whole series of clicks, as the Master turned the Key first one way and then the other, like someone manipulating a particularly intricate combination lock. With each series of turns the black rod slid further into the hole, until with a final click it disappeared completely. The Master scurried back, as the whole central area of the dais slid away, and a strange shape emerged ... It was a shining monolith, a pillar almost as tall as a man. It might have been carved from one enormous black diamond. The pillar was throbbing with unimaginable power. Six gleaming metallic coils ran from its base, and disappeared into the depths from which it had emerged.

The Master looked at the monolith. Even he was awed. 'Rassilon's Star!' he murmured. 'The Eye of Harmony . . .'

The Doctor and Spandrell were leaning exhausted by the vault door. They had heaved at the iron shutter until their muscles creaked, but nothing happened.

'It's no use,' said Engin despairingly. 'You'll never shift it!'

The Doctor straightened up and prowled restlessly around the vault. 'We've got to get out . . .' He paused by the far corner, and looked up. 'There's some kind of shaft over here . . . and a gleam of light at the top. Where does it lead?'

Spandrell peered upwards. 'To the Panopticon, I imagine. Looks like an old service shaft.'

'If you can get me into it, I can chimney myself up to the top.'

Engin looked up in horror. 'It's a hundred feet high, at least, Doctor. If you slip . . .'

The Doctor ignored him. 'Come on, Spandrell. If we drag the empty bier over to this corner . . . You get on, and I'll stand on your shoulders . . .' A faint rumble of power shook the vault.

'What was that?' asked Engin apprehensively.

'The Master at work, I should imagine. Now come on, Spandrell, there's no time to waste.'

It didn't take the Master long to remember that he had come, not to admire the Eye of Harmony, but to steal it. Settling the gleaming Sash of Rassilon about his shoulders, to protect him from the monolith's energy-field, he began uncoupling the first of the six coils. As he freed the link and withdrew it, there was a deep ominous rumbling from the chasm below the monolith. Already the energy-balance had been disturbed.

Back against one wall, legs against the other, the Doctor edged his way slowly up the smooth metal shaft. He seemed to have been climbing forever. He paused to rest, and great drops of sweat splashed from his forehead and trickled down his nose. Far below he could just see the faces of Spandrell and Engin, peering anxiously up the shaft. Above was only the tiny gleam of light that never seemed to get any nearer. The whole Panopticon was rumbling and shaking now, and so was the Doctor's shaft. Legs and back aching, eyes blinded with sweat, the Doctor continued his climb.

Working his way round the monolith, the Master was disconnecting one energy coil after another. As the imbalance of forces grew steadily greater, the rumbling from the chasm grew louder. The monolith itself began to hum with energy ... An earthquake-like tremor rocked the Panopticon, and an ominous crack appeared in the rear wall ...

The tremor almost shook the Doctor out of his shaft. He did actually slip back a few feet, then managed to brace himself again, thrusting legs and back against the vibrating sides of the shaft. The shaking lessened and he resumed his agonising climb.

Spandrell pulled Engin out of the way as a chunk of masonry crashed down from the ceiling. The whole vault was shaking. Engin looked at Spandrell in alarm. 'What is it? What's happening?'

'If the Doctor's right,' said Spandrell grimly, 'it's the beginning of the end of the world ...'

The Doctor was nearly at the top now. The shaft ended in a metal grille. Bracing himself awkwardly he kicked upwards with his right foot until the grille came free. The Doctor struggled through the gap and found he'd emerged through the floor of one of the Panopticon's outer corridors. The whole building was rumbling and shaking, and seemed about to fall on his head at any moment. Piercing through all the noise was a high-pitched whine of pure energy. The Doctor began running towards the sound.

Only two of the energy coils were connected now, and a storm of pure energy coming from the monolith was fast wrecking not only the Panopticon but most of the city around it. From outside the Panopticon came screams of terror and the crash of falling masonry.

The Master laughed. He paused to rest for a moment, clinging to the vibrating monolith. The effect of the contact with the energy-source was immediate and extraordinary. His limbs grew strong again, his back straightened. When he spoke, his voice had its old resonance. 'Rassilon's discovery,' he roared. 'All mine!' He hugged the monolith exultantly. 'When I bear this back to my TARDIS, it will give me supreme power over the Universe. I shall be Master of all matter!'

Moving quickly and confidently now, he bent to remove another coil. The coil came free, there was a sound like breaking ice and big cracks appeared in the Panopticon floor ...

As the Doctor ran into the hall a huge section of floor simply vanished before his feet, crashing away into nothingness. Jumping back, the Doctor skirted his way round the chasm and ran across the rapidly-crumbling floor. He arrived on the central dais, just as the Master bent to uncouple the final coil. 'Stop!' he shouted.

The Master looked up from his task. He seemed almost pleased to see the Doctor. 'Congratulations! You are just in time for the end!'

He began to uncouple the last energy coil.

'Don't!' shouted the Doctor. 'Unscrew that and you'll die as surely as any of us.'

The Master smiled and shook his head. 'You can do better than that, Doctor. I am wearing the Sash of Rassilon.' He touched the gleaming band of metal across his chest.

'So was the President when he was shot down. The

117

staser-bolt damaged the Sash. It won't protect you now—it's useless! Look!' and the Doctor pointed.

'You lie,' screamed the Master, but for a second he glanced down. In that second the Doctor hurled himself across the dais in an incredible flying tackle. They went down together in a tangle of arms and legs, rolling across the shuddering floor.

Despairingly the Doctor realised how much contact with the Eye of Harmony had restored the Master's strength. The scrawny limbs beneath his grip felt like coiled steel. With a savage heave the Master threw the Doctor from him, and bent to complete the uncoupling of the last energy-coil. As his hands closed on the connection, the Doctor scrabbled desperately across the floor and dragged him away. He pulled the Master to his feet and they grappled fiercely for a moment. Once again, the Master's new-found strength came to his aid. He flung the Doctor aside almost with ease, sprang back towards the monolith—and stumbled on a chunk of loose rubble. His foot twisted and he fell helplessly backwards. Arms flailing he pitched clear off the dais—and into the spreading chasm in the Panopticon floor ... For a moment the Master clutched desperately at the edge of the chasm, hanging on by two claw-like hands. Then the masonry crumbled away beneath his grip, and he fell screaming to the depths below.

The Doctor picked himself up, and began re-coupling energy-coils with frantic speed. As one coil after another was linked back into place, the sub-terranean rumbling steadied, diminished, and gradually died away ... Gallifrey had been saved.

12

An End—and a Beginning

The Chancellery office had lost much of its former opulence. Half the roof had fallen in and there was dust and rubble everywhere.

With a gesture of irritation, Cardinal Borusa swept some chunks of loose masonry from his desk. 'Half the city in ruins, untold damage. Countless lives lost . . .'

Engin nodded sympathetically. 'Quite so, Cardinal. Had it not been for the Doctor, it could have been much worse.'

'Yes, indeed, I am quite conscious of the debt we owe.' Borusa glanced a little awkwardly at the Doctor who had recovered his own clothes from the museum case, and was happily winding his incredibly long scarf around his neck.

'Nevertheless,' Borusa continued gloomily. 'This is still the greatest catastrophe Gallifrey has ever known. What will we tell the people? What can we *say*?'

The Doctor rose, tilting his hat to a jaunty angle. 'You'll just have to adjust the truth again, Cardinal. How about, oh I don't know . . . Subsidence owing to a plague of very large mice?'

Worn and harried as he was, Borusa still wasn't going to tolerate cheek from his old pupil. 'I believe I told you long ago, Doctor, you will never amount to anything in the galaxy while you retain your propensity for vulgar facetiousness.'

For a moment the Doctor was back in the Academy again—then he grinned unabashed. 'Yes, sir, you did tell me that. Many times! Can I go now, sir?'

'Indeed you can, Doctor—preferably with the utmost despatch. Perhaps you will see that the transduction barriers are raised, Castellan?'

Spandrell had been watching them both with some apprehension. 'Of course, sir.' A little hurriedly, he ushered the Doctor towards the door.

As they reached it, Borusa called, 'Oh, Doctor?'

The Doctor turned. 'Yes, sir?'

There was the ghost of a smile on the Cardinal's face—he might almost have been feeling proud of his old pupil. 'Nine out of ten, Doctor.'

The Doctor smiled. 'Thank you, sir,' he said respectfully, and left.

Key in hand, the Doctor stood outside the TARDIS. Spandrell and Engin beside him. 'You know, Doctor, if you *wanted* to stay,' said Engin wistfully, 'I'm sure any past difficulties could be overlooked.'

The Doctor looked affectionately down at the old Co-ordinator. How could he make the old Time Lord understand ... 'No, I don't think I will, thanks all the same. Believe it or not, I actually like it out there.' He turned to the Castellan. 'Thank you, Spandrell— for trusting me.'

'It's we who should thank you, Doctor. You destroyed the Master.'

'I didn't actually *see* him die, you know. I was rather busy.'

Engin shuddered. 'But even if he did survive the fall—wasn't he dying anyway?'

The Doctor stared abstractedly at an ornate grandfather clock which stood near the TARDIS. 'There was a lot of energy coming from that monolith. The Sash of Rassilon might have enabled him to convert it.'

'You're not suggesting he's still alive?' asked Spandrell incredulously.

'I hope not. And there's no one else in all the galaxies I'd say that about. He's the quintessence of evil.' The Doctor had always hated farewells. Abruptly he said, 'Well, goodbye to you both,' and disappeared inside the TARDIS.

Spandrell and Engin stepped back as the TARDIS dematerialisation noise began. Seconds later the TARDIS had faded away.

They were about to go when they heard *another dematerialisation noise*. It seemed to be coming from the grandfather clock. For a moment the clock-face turned into a familiar skull-like face, lips curled in a mocking smile.

'Look,' shouted Spandrell. 'It's the Master!' He drew his staser-pistol but the clock had vanished.

Spandrell sighed, and holstered the staser. 'Too late —they've gone.'

Engin was considerably put out at this further

upset. '*Where* have they gone?' he demanded peevishly. 'Where do you think they're heading?'

Spandrell gestured expansively. 'Out into the Universe, Co-ordinator. And you know—I've a feeling it isn't big enough for both of them!'